ORC EROICA

Conjecture Chronicles

4

"Sometimes, I miss the war. We could capture as many men as we wanted and devour their essence as we pleased..."

Carrot

A succubus who bears the title Breathstealer. She's Bash's old war buddy and was an elite member of the succubus army.

Carrot

Silviana

Silviana

Fifth-born beastkin princess. She has declared her love for Bash, the man who killed her uncle, the Hero Leto, and is actively pursuing him.

"You impossible man... You mean to suggest that I'm the after-dinner dessert?"

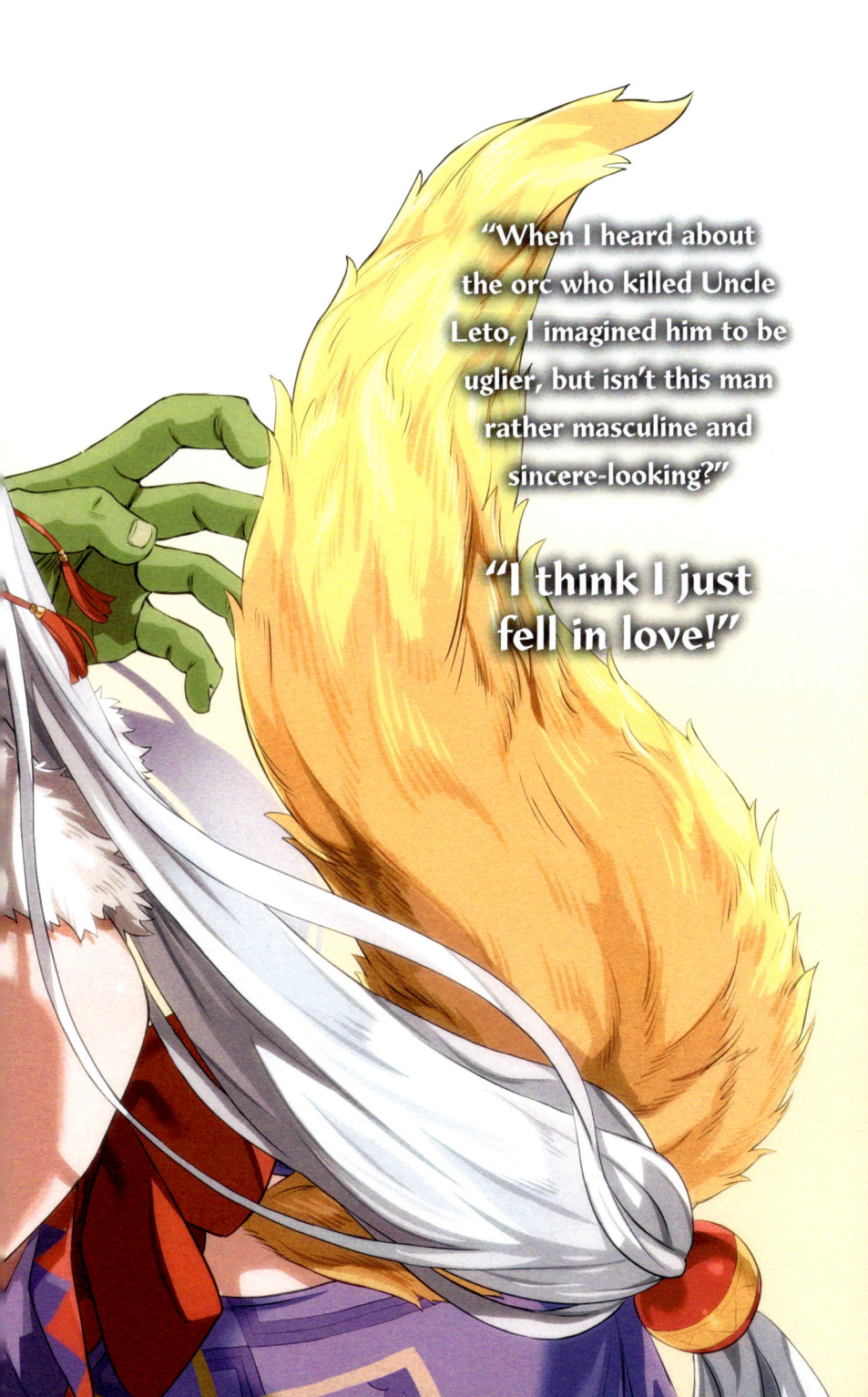

"When I heard about the orc who killed Uncle Leto, I imagined him to be uglier, but isn't this man rather masculine and sincere-looking?"

"I think I just fell in love!"

ORC EROICA

CONTENTS

Book Four: Beastkin Country / The Lycant Saga

ORC EROICA

CONJECTURE CHRONICLES

4

Rifujin na Magonote

Illustration by
Asanagi

YEN ON

New York

ORC EROICA 4

Rifujin na Magonote

Translation by Evie Lund
Cover art by Asanagi

This book is a work of fiction. Names, characters, places, and incidents are the product of the author's imagination or are used fictitiously. Any resemblance to actual events, locales, or persons, living or dead, is coincidental.

ORC EIYU MONOGATARI Volume 4 SONTAKU RETSUDEN
©Rifujin na Magonote, Asanagi 2022
First published in Japan in 2022 by KADOKAWA CORPORATION, Tokyo.
English translation rights arranged with KADOKAWA CORPORATION, Tokyo through
TUTTLE-MORI AGENCY, INC., Tokyo.

English translation © 2024 by Yen Press, LLC

Yen On
150 West 30th Street, 19th Floor
New York, NY 10001

Visit us at yenpress.com
facebook.com/yenpress
twitter.com/yenpress
yenpress.tumblr.com
instagram.com/yenpress

First Yen On Edition: March 2024
Edited by Yen On Editorial: Payton Campbell
Designed by Yen Press Design: Wendy Chan

Yen On is an imprint of Yen Press, LLC.
The Yen On name and logo are trademarks of Yen Press, LLC.

The publisher is not responsible for websites (or their content) that are not owned by the publisher.

Library of Congress Cataloging-in-Publication Data
Names: Na Magonote, Rifujin, author. | Asanagi, illustrator. | Lund, Evie, translator.
Title: Orc eroica / Rifujin na Magonote ; illustration by Asanagi ; translated by Evie Lund.
Other titles: Orc eiyuu monogatari. English
Description: First Yen On edition. | New York, NY : Yen On, 2021–
Identifiers: LCCN 2021038197 | ISBN 9781975334338 (v. 1 ; trade paperback) |
    ISBN 9781975343040 (v. 2 ; trade paperback) | ISBN 9781975348472 (v. 3 ; trade paperback) |
    ISBN 9781975391485 (v. 4 ; trade paperback)
Subjects: LCGFT: Fantasy fiction. | Light novels.
Classification: LCC PL873.5.A17 O7313 2021 | DDC 895.63/6—dc23
LC record available at https://lccn.loc.gov/2021038197

ISBNs: 978-1-9753-9148-5 (paperback)
    978-1-9753-9149-2 (ebook)

10 9 8 7 6 5 4 3 2 1

LBK

Printed in the United States of America

忖度 (*sontaku*) "conjecture, surmise"; to make an assumption or guess about the feelings of another, and to then demonstrate care or consideration for the other party based on this.

(Source: Wikipedia Japan)

Book Four

The Lycant Saga

Beastkin Country

EROICA

1

†HE GONGLASHA MOUNTAINS

If you moved northwest along the mountains from Mount Rind, you would find yourself in the Gonglasha Mountains.

A mountain range, comprising Mount Gongol, Mount Graat, and Mount Alyosha, reaching an altitude of thirteen thousand feet.

And beyond that mountain range? Beastkin country.

The Gonglasha Mountains were dwarf territory, but not all mountains had holes through them like at Dobanga Pit, which led to the other side. Even if a route through to the beastkin country existed, that didn't necessarily mean it would be common knowledge. And of course, it wouldn't show on any map.

Therefore, if a traveler wanted to move from the dwarf country to the beastkin country, they would have to make a detour around this vast mountain range. After all, the mountain range was very steep and not a place that was well suited for people to pass through.

"Seems the fog is getting thicker."

"You're right."

And yet, on this mountain, we find…Bash.

The Orc Hero.

Accustomed to harsh battlefields, he occasionally traversed rugged mountain roads like this, not to mention dense forests and battlefields awash with magic spells. With his strong orc body and inexhaustible physical strength, crossing this mountain range was a piece of cake for Bash.

"Can you still see the ground below?"

"I can, but it matters not."

Bash was now hanging on to a sheer cliff face in dense fog.

Yes, he clung to the steep slope but moved at a high speed without any regard for the danger, just like a giant spider.

Any who did not know him would blink and rub their eyes at such a sight. They might pinch their cheeks, wondering if they were being tricked by some sort of creature that cast magical illusions.

But those who knew Bash would merely nod at such a sight. *Ah yes, that's Bash*, they'd say. *Tripping along a sheer and treacherous cliff at a brisk clip.*

"Hmm? Say, Boss, you're in a good mood. What's up?"

"Just the thought of beastkin women."

Bash wore a silly smile.

He was thinking of the beastkin women he'd seen during the war. All fierce warriors with supple and beautiful bodies.

The beastkin.

If you want them summed up in a simple term, let's go with: *bipedal beasts*.

Agile and ferocious. Ruthless with a cruel nature. They can see in the dark, and even in dense fog, they can detect their enemies with their keen sense of smell.

And the pièce de résistance? They can communicate with their fellows using a special cry audible only to them. With this, they can corner an enemy in a showy siege attack. They pale in comparison to other races when it comes to magic, but what do they care?

They're a *warrior* race, after all.

That said, there is another important piece of trivia about them as far as the orcs are concerned.

Beastkin are multiparous.

A single pregnancy can yield anywhere from three to seven children.

On top of that, during the mating season, which occurs once a year, the beastkin women get frisky. They'll shack up with anyone, even an orc. In fact, sometimes they themselves are the sexual aggressors.

Because of this, beastkin ladies were extremely popular with some orcs.

Yes, if you were dead set on having children, a beastkin partner was a fine choice.

As for their looks... Well, opinion is divided among orcs. But it's really a matter of personal preference. And compared to the dwarves, there's quite a disparity from beastkin to beastkin.

When Bash imagined meeting a beastkin woman the likes of which he'd still never seen, his jaw slackened, and his steps grew bouncier.

"This time, I want to find a wife."

"That's right! Up until now, I've been overwhelmed by half-baked information, and so I can't really say with confidence I was able to provide adequate support. But this time, I'll help you find the perfect partner!"

Three failed proposals.

The veteran warrior, Bash, was beginning to grow just a tad impatient.

Sure, he still had some time until he turned the big 3-0, but not much. There was no time for dawdling around.

If the worst happened, Bash would be...finished. He would have to spend the rest of his days skulking in the dark.

The royal beastkin engagement.

The whole of beastkin country, aflutter because of it.

What kind of Hero...? What kind of veteran warrior would Bash be if he failed to capitalize on this golden opportunity?

This time, the two were in better spirits than ever before.

"Hey, which way is it?"

After passing over the precipice and straightening his posture, Bash surveyed the area. They may have been in high spirits, but that didn't change the fact that it was dense fog as far as the eye could see.

It was only just possible to tell which way was up and which way was down.

"This way! This way! The Red Forest is definitely over here! Trust me, Boss, and follow me!"

"Right!"

Luckily, Bash had a fairy companion who was a master of reconnaissance.

Anyone unfamiliar with the fairy named Zell might have been doubtful of their outlandish proclamations and behaviors and thus been inclined to take the wrong path.

But Bash and Zell were old friends. Whether in a strange forest drenched in thunderstorms, in swamps piled with corpses, or on battlefields ringing with steel against steel, Bash had always believed in Zell's advice, followed it, and survived.

And he would continue to trust them.

Indeed, sometimes there were long detours. But Bash knew they would always reach their destination.

Rugged bare rock surface. The air, thin and cold, and given the season, snow was to be expected.

A harsh environment, one where a human would freeze to death in an instant. But Bash's steps were light. Because the beastkin country...the Red Forest...was just around the corner.

"Hmm? The fog is clearing!"

Just then, a strong breeze blew.

The fog began to clear, carried away by the wind.

Light shone through the clouds that covered the sky, and the sky itself seemed to open up.

It all happened in the space of about one minute.

The fog around Bash cleared, the sky was cloudless, and the sun was now shining brightly.

"This is what they call cloudbreak, huh?"

In the continent of Vastonia, the weather had a habit of changing suddenly.

When heavy rain or a storm suddenly stops and the sky clears up, that's called a cloudbreak, and when heavy rain or a storm suddenly occurs, it's called a cloudburst.

They often happened in the midst of big battles and somewhat turned the tide of the fight, history says.

Even Bash had experience with cloudbreaks and cloudbursts.

Even in that unforgettable decisive battle on the Remium Plateau, there had been cloudbreaks and cloudbursts.

But they were no product of nature...

"Oh, over there! The beastkin forest is over there!"

Just as Bash was about to recall a certain...individual, Zell cried out.

Where Zell was pointing—to the rear and to the right—a red forest was visible, just below the precipice they had just passed through. A large forest, with bright-red autumn leaves. The beastkin's Red Forest.

"Come on, let's go down!"

"Right!"

It was back the way they had come, slightly, but Bash wasn't about to split hairs.

It was always like this when he let Zell navigate. Ultimately, all Bash cared about was arriving at his destination in a timely manner. So there was no problem. And if he traveled alone, there was a chance he wouldn't make it at all. Or if he did, he might arrive far too late.

They began descending the steep slope with a *crunch* of loose stones.

Orcs who knew Bash well would nod at such a sight and say, *Yes, that's Bash. Always prudent. Wouldn't just come charging down.*

"...Hmm?"

On the way down the slope, Bash suddenly felt a presence and looked back.

"..."

Turning around, he saw the summit.

The top of the mountain range seemed far away, even with Bash's keen eyesight.

There, something glittered and reflected the light.

It was hard to see because of the sun in the backdrop, but upon looking closely, he could see someone standing there.

"What's wrong, Boss?"

"...It's nothing. It seems there were other travelers lost in the fog besides us."

Still, Bash was an orc.

Orcs didn't quibble over small things. What did it matter if there was someone standing at the top?

"Hmm. I see."

And Zell wasn't the type to pay attention to small details, either.

(Right?)

For a moment, Bash summoned the name of that particular individual... But then he quickly shook his head.

That person wasn't the type to rough it in the mountains. And even if they were here...it was no concern of Bash's.

"Well, first off, we need to find the border checkpoint! Let's go!"

"Right!"

And so the two of them went down the mountain.

■

"It's a rogue orc! A rogue orc has appeared!"

"All units, ready your weapons! In the name of the former Dog Corps, leave none alive!"

"Do not let the princess's shining day be besmirched!"

As Bash approached the border, a fuss and a clamor started up.

Bulldog-faced soldiers, ones who had fought and survived combat countless times, surrounded Bash with their fangs bared.

"Wait, I'm not a rogue orc. My name is Bash, and I'm traveling in search of something!"

"That's right! Why, you won't find a rogue orc that's got this kind of dignity! Behold the skin of this orc, which has been polished to a sheen by daily bathing... Er, all right, it's a little dirty because we went over the mountains today. But give him a whiff! He smells like a meadow! ...Erm, all right, so he smells just a bit ripe, but that's because we just crossed a mountain! His face, then! Behold the boss's mug! So refined, not like a rogue orc at all! And his tusks! Are they not splendid?!"

The bulldog soldiers looked puzzled by the fairy zooming around in the air and jabbering away at the speed of light, but they did not lower their swords.

In fact, once they heard the name Bash, their frowns grew sterner.

"Bash? You mean the Orc Hero Bash?!"

"The very same!"

"You! What's your business in this land?!"

"I heard the third-born princess of this country is getting married."

The moment Bash said that, the hair of the leading soldier in the pack suddenly stood on end. Then he seemed to radiate murderous intent. With bloodthirsty eyes, he pointed his sword at Bash.

"You! You slipped through our net!"

"You shall not pass!"

"We'll kill you, even if it costs our lives!"

Usually, Bash had only one response when faced with a bloodthirsty opponent wielding a sword.

To fight.

He would draw the sword slung on his back, mow down everything in sight, and break right through. Then he'd continue about his business.

"Hmm..."

But Bash did not draw his weapon.

He knew brandishing his sword here would bring him no closer to his goal.

"What? What's all this about? You're saying he can't pass because he's an orc?! Show me the documentation where it says that! You can't because there isn't any! By the laws of peacetime, you are duty bound to allow safe passage to any traveler! Are you sure you wanna do this?! You want everyone to think the beastkin believe themselves above the rules of social discourse?! You really want to lower your status like that, hmm?!"

"Who cares about treaties?!"

Even Zell's impassioned speech failed to sway them.

Everyone was glaring at Bash with open hostility and murderous intent.

A fight was about to kick off at any moment.

From the looks of them, they were veteran warriors. And they seemed to know of Bash. Bash did not know them...but there was no doubt he'd faced them in battle before. It was highly likely that he'd even killed some of their comrades.

Those were the vibes they were giving off.

But now was a time of peace.

Nonaggression was the common desire.

Even those who held grudges ought to have held those grudges against war itself, not the races they fought during that period.

However, not everyone could see reason.

And sometimes, confronted with the slayer of their parents and siblings, rationality flew out the window.

But perhaps it was precisely because they knew of Bash that they had not yet attacked.

Because they knew that if they jumped into a conflict, he could very well turn them into mincemeat.

"Hmm... Can you let me through?"

Bash was at a loss.

Now that he thought about it, though he'd endured rejection and looks of suspicion, he had never been denied a border crossing before. Sure, he'd faced resistance from time to time. But this was the first time he'd seen such blatant murderous intent.

"..."

Bash had no intention of fighting.

Nonetheless, if they really wanted to swing down those raised swords...

...even Bash would be compelled to fight.

Fleeing from battle is not an option for a proud orc warrior.

Even more so if the other party is also proud and comes at him with this amount of seriousness.

Bash did not move.

If he took even one step forward, they would attack.

If he reached for the sword on his back, they would attack.

Or even if Bash turned on his heel and started walking back the way he had come, they might seize the opportunity to attack him.

And in that moment, Bash's plan to find a wife in the beastkin country would melt away like pond scum.

Bash had no plan B.

His hopes of finding a bride would be dashed, and he would remain a virgin.

The final result...wizardification. And with that badge of dishonor upon his forehead, Bash would lose everything.

He was getting desperate.

Come to think of it, this might have been the toughest spot Bash had ever been in.

"Hmm, hmm, hmm. ♪ Hmm, hmm, hmm. ♪ Hmm, hmm, HMM. ♪ Hmm, hmm, hmm. ♪ Hmm, hmm, hmm. ♪ Hmm, hmm, HMM. ♪"

Just then...

There came the sound of...humming.

And not just humming, but the twanging of some kind of string instrument also. Like a cross between a cat's yowl and the screech of a hellbird... But definitely some sort of musical instrument.

Just behind Bash...

"...!"

Bash, honestly, expected it.

I mean, borders tended to be hotspots for significant encounters, at least as far as he was concerned.

He'd met Thunder Sonia in the Shiwanashi Forest, and he'd met Primera at Dobanga Pit.

Both of them had turned down his proposals, yes, but they were beautiful women, and Bash would have been more than satisfied with either one.

So a part of him swelled with anticipation that maybe this time, too...

"Hmm, hmm, hmm. ♪ Hmm, hmm, hmm. ♪ Hmm, hmm, HMM. ♪ HEY! ♪"

The hummer passed by Bash and whirled around in the space between him and the soldiers.

With a cry, the hummer pointed at the sky.

Bash was disappointed.

The hummer was a man.

"Is there a problem here?"

He pointed his finger at the soldiers and spoke in a familiar tone, as if he was talking to old friends of about ten years' acquaintance.

He was incredibly frank.

"..."

Confusion transcends race.

After exchanging a glance with Zell, Bash looked at the beastkin soldiers.

Did they know this hummer? No, that wasn't the case.

Bash couldn't read minds or anything, but he didn't need to in this scenario. It was that obvious. He fixed his eyes on the hummer again.

The man appeared to be human.

But not a woman, sadly. He carried the sort of string instrument popular with humans and wore a mask designed to resemble a woman's face.

Highly suspicious.

"...I want to pass, but they won't listen to reason."

Bash spoke plainly. It was his way of answering the man's question.

The man whirled to face Bash.

"You don't say?"

"I do."

Then he turned to the soldiers.

"You don't say?"

"We are members of the former Dog Corps. And this...*this*...is the Orc Hero Bash. We cannot permit him to pass."

When he heard that, the man spread his arms wider and spoke as if appealing to the soldiers.

"I understand how you feel!"

He spun around with his hands raised up high and spoke in a theatrical tone.

"I also lost someone important to me in the war! If I said I didn't still hold a grudge against the one who did it, I'd be a liar!"

Then he stopped in his tracks.

"However! In this peaceful age, that way of thinking is not good!"

"..."

"You people may have lost someone like that in the war, too! But think about it. We, the Alliance of Four, have made peace. And why? Because after suffering through all that strife, we decided we didn't want to lose any more loved ones! Do you not now have people you hold dear? When you return home tonight, will you not be returning to the ones you love?"

"However!" said the man with a theatrical gesture, holding aloft his stringed instrument, and from it there issued a heavy clunking sound.

It was a clumsy, unsophisticated sort of sound, like something unpleasant being suddenly exposed.

The soldiers wondered how such a harsh sound could issue from an ordinary stringed instrument.

"This gentleman is also a veteran warrior! If you fight, one or two of you may die. Or you may all die! Now, of course, I'm not making light of your martial skills. But such is war! And if you die, those waiting for you at home will weep and wail and gnash their teeth. And the hopes of those who dream of peace will be dashed... Dashed, I say!"

The stringed instrument made another booming sound.

The sound was so unpleasant that some of the men had to cover their ears.

"As an emissary of love and peace, I cannot overlook this! So even if I lose face, let it be on my good honor, and allow this man safe passage!"

The man spread his arms wide again as he spoke.

The soldiers looked at one another.

The man's face was covered with a mask, and yet he spoke of losing face? Of his honor?

"Get outta here! Who the hell are you anyway?"

"...Oops, that's right. I forgot to introduce myself."

The man cleared his throat with a *harrumph!*

He took out something that looked like a letter from his pocket and handed it to the soldier.

"What is this...? What?!"

The change in the expression of the soldier who saw it was dramatic.

"You... I mean, Your Greatness...!"

The man gently placed his hand over the soldier's mouth.

"Shhh," he hissed, through his teeth.

"But why...? Why the mask?"

"To protect the peace of the world... These days, I am a messenger of the peace."

As he spoke, the man picked up his stringed instrument and plucked it again.

The soldiers flinched, but only slightly.

Bash and Zell did not know the particulars of the letter the man carried, nor his identity.

But he seemed to be someone very important from the way the soldiers were reacting.

"I don't really understand the specifics, but are you saying you don't want a grand welcome or something like that?"

"Precisely that."

The soldier returned the letter to the man and frowned.

"But this is a golden day for the royal princess... I cannot permit the Orc Hero Bash to enter..."

"I understand your concern...but I think the princess's special day is exactly the kind of day for letting an Orc Hero enter."

"..."

"What? He won't do anything. The fact that you pointed your sword at him and he didn't draw his sword is proof of that. And him being the orc he is, too. If you're not convinced, I will vouch for him. He's no threat to the beastkin race. I assure you."

The man turned to Bash as if to say, *Isn't that right?*

"You won't do anything untoward, will you?"

"Correct. I'm not here to cause any trouble."

Bash nodded.

Of course, he had no intention of causing trouble. He hadn't had any major problems in towns up until now, and he planned to do well in this town of the beastkin.

"See? He swears it himself."

"...We cannot trust the word of an orc... But if *you* say so, we will obey your word."

The soldiers were not afraid that Bash would cause trouble.

They had another reason.

"But if anything happens, we'll do our best to hunt down the orc."

"Well, I'll just have to hope that doesn't happen."

The man—the emissary of love and peace—nodded in satisfaction as he spoke.

■   ■   ■

"Thank you for the help."

After passing through the checkpoint, Bash spoke to the emissary.

Without his intervention, it would have rained blood at the checkpoint.

And after that, getting access to the country would have been a joke of a prospect. Worse yet, the incident might've sparked another war.

"That's fine! After all, I am... Er, I am Errol, the emissary of love and peace!"

The emissary of love and peace spoke while plucking his stringed instrument.

It sounded a bit like the groans Bash had overheard when an orc warlord was taking a woman in his hut.

Bash didn't know much about music, but it felt to him like the sound of hope.

It made Bash hope that he, too, could produce that kind of sound in the future.

"And it is right that you should come..."

"What?"

"No, it's nothing! Ah-ha-ha-ha-ha!"

Errol suddenly burst out laughing and rushed off.

"Well, let's meet again!"

"Right! I'll repay the favor, sooner or later!"

"Ha-ha, I'm looking forward to it, Orc Hero Bash!"

Errol laughed as he ran down the road into town.

Same destination. If so, there would probably be an opportunity for them to meet again.

"Wow, he sure liked to talk a lot."

"Indeed."

Not that Zell was really one to talk, but Bash decided to agree with the fairy anyway.

Bash had not met a man much like that in his travels thus far. But then Bash paused, and a thoughtful expression crossed his face. An expression that orcs don't often show, as if he was exploring the depths of memory.

"Huh? Boss, something bothering you?"

"...I think I've met that man somewhere before."

"What, like, on the battlefield?"

But the man Bash recalled had been more put together than that foppish demeanor.

At first glance, he looked like he had many weaknesses, but both Bash and Zell could instinctively see that no true gap existed in his armor. A veteran warrior...and it was clear that he must have been a person of some importance.

But Bash had no recollection of the nickname emissary of love and peace, of the mask he wore, or of the name Errol.

Not to mention the stringed instrument.

"Well, more importantly, I'll go forth and do my best to find a wife this time!"

"Yes! That's right!"

If they couldn't place the man, then that was that.

Bash and Zell were not the types to fuss over details.

Right now, they were merely excited to enter the beastkin country.

2

BLY MONTHLY

The beastkin country. The Red Forest.

A beautiful place.

Trees with red and yellow leaves growing in clusters and all manner of animals contributing to the ecosystem. Here, you could find the true essence of Mother Earth, a presence that gave comfort to all.

In the center of the forest stood a huge tree, a tree that was said to have stood before the war.

The beastkin tribe called the giant tree the Sacred Tree and called this forest the Sacred Land.

This place was very special to the beastkin.

About one hundred years ago, the beastkin were robbed of their holy land.

It happened only a few years after Geddigs had been crowned Demon Lord.

At that time, Geddigs had the beastkin on the ropes. Many races had been on the brink of extinction during the war and the beastkin were no exception. After his accession to the throne, Geddigs focused on the beastkin and tried to annihilate them.

Even as he held back the other races, he attacked the beastkin race most fiercely and tried to rob them of their power.

He must have assumed that if he could destroy even one of the races belonging to the Alliance of Four, he would claim victory.

The beastkin were deprived of 80 percent of their territory and population and driven to the remote Green Forest. Without the invaluable support of the elves and the dwarves, the beastkin race might have been completely wiped out.

The beastkin recaptured their holy land several years before Geddigs died.

This victory was the work of an army of beastkin who had amassed their strength in the Green Forest.

Leto Rivergold was the author of that triumph.

A son of the Rivergolds, the royal family of the beastkin.

Having earned the title of the strongest of the beastkin, he led a mighty army to invade and recapture the Red Forest.

Praised for his achievements and courage, he was given the title of Hero by the king.

The Beastkin Hero, Leto.

The recapture of the Red Forest went down in beastkin history as the only battle in which Geddigs was dealt a painful blow.

However, for the Coalition of Seven, which had already taken control of the Gonglasha Mountains, the Red Forest had no strategic value left, so it was not a major loss for Geddigs. That was likely why he had conceded it so easily. Or at least, that was the opinion held by the other races.

That's not to say there wasn't loss involved.

After all, the beastkin regained their fighting spirit by recapturing the Red Forest.

For a hundred years, the beastkin, who'd until then lived like neutered cats, lived instead as fierce territorial tigers that protected their territory.

"This place takes me back!"

"You said it, Boss."

Incidentally, Bash had been present during that battle.

It was a bitter defeat of a battle, one that took place when Bash was still a young orc, wet behind the ears.

The air was thick with the stench of blood, there were enemy soldiers everywhere, and the fighting was constant. Bash had still been a weak pup at the time and was probably just lucky to have made it through with his hide intact.

You might even say that Bash's true war career began right here, in this forest.

His first battle wasn't here, true, but this was where he had tasted his first defeat.

"Man, just thinkin' back on it is enough to have me pissing my fairy pants! Beastkin eat fairies, after all."

"Are you referencing Gordon the Fairy Eater?"

"Yeah, him! Just reliving it is enough to give me goose bumps! That damned gourmand! After wrapping me up in a roll, he smeared honey all over me and then put mustard on top of the honey! *Mustard* on top of *honey*?! Then, after licking me for a taste test, he had the audacity to say, 'Eugh, gross,' and tossed me away! I practically fainted! There's no way honey and mustard would go together! Right?!"

Zell was a fairy of advanced age.

Even since meeting Bash as a new recruit, Zell had been a veteran warrior and had freely earned the nickname of Zell the Mercy Beggar.

And Gordon the Fairy Eater was a beastkin warrior.

As the name suggests, he was an adventurous eater who was famous for catching and eating fairies.

Zell had once been captured by Gordon.

But why was Zell not eaten?

The reason is simple.

Before a beastkin eats something, they lick it with the tip of their tongue to see if it's poisonous.

According to Gordon, fairy skin tastes sweet like nectar.

However, that day, Zell had already survived many days of fierce battle and was in a very foul mood.

Thus, Zell was covered in that *particular fairy substance.*

Gordon's tongue became numb after just that one lick, his vision swam, and he fainted like a harpy.

The next day, he was awoken by intense vomiting and violent diarrhea.

The beastkin, who'd developed a taste for fairy flesh, were terrified by Gordon's culinary report.

And Zell gained another nickname...Gutwrecker Zell.

It was a shameful nickname for Zell, perhaps, but the fairies lauded Zell as a hero.

After that day, the number of fairies eaten by Gordon decreased sharply.

"But you know, the Red Forest in peacetime is nice. The air is clean, it's quiet, it's peaceful, and the sunlight filtering through the trees stimulates my fairy senses. I feel great!"

"Indeed."

The two only knew of the Red Forest as a fiercely contested area.

Back in the day, it was impossible to differentiate between the redness of the autumn leaves and those painted red with blood.

Most of the trees were charred black, and the ground was never dry, always slippery and slick with blood.

You might even have assumed that the name Red Forest was because it was raining blood there all the time.

Who could have thought it would become such a quiet, serene place…?

"Hmm?"

Suddenly, a rustling sound underfoot startled them from their ruminations.

"Hmm? What's this? Trash?"

When Bash lifted his leg, the object that was stuck there fell to the ground with a *floomp*.

It was a stack of dirty paper.

"Tsk! Just because it's peacetime, that doesn't mean we can start littering! The bones of great heroes rest in this forest! And the beastkin… They fought hard to reclaim this place! It's disrespectful to the heroic spirits, ain't it, Boss? …Hmm?"

"What is it?"

"Hmm… It's a magazine… Check this out!"

Zell lifted into the air a magazine that was as tall as them and read the article titles.

"'Six Rules to Capture His Heart'…!"

"'How to Choose a Marriage Partner You Won't Regret for the Rest of Your Life'!"

"'Common Sense to Be Popular with Girls, 100 Hot Tips'!"

"'Beastkin Love and Marriage Values No One Tells You About These Days'!"

"'Cool Outfit Choices for Marriage Seekers…Guy Edition'…!"

Yep, it was a magazine, all right.

"*Bly Monthly!*"

"…What is that?"

"Don't you know?! It's a magazine published by the great human merchant Bly after the war!"

"A maga...zine?"

"It's a bundle of papers that summarizes the news of each country and the interests of the people!"

"Such a thing exists...?"

Naturally, there was nothing like that in orc territory.

There wasn't really a place for things like art and literature in orc culture.

"And this is a special issue about love and marriage!"

"What does that mean?"

"Harrumph! Boss, don't play dumb! What I'm saying is, this contains a lot of information about love and marriage collected by the great merchant Bly!"

"So it's credible?"

"Of course! Speaking of Bly, he's a former elite of the Human Intelligence Department!"

"Oh, *that* Bly!"

The average human was physically weaker than the average beastkin or dwarf.

Their magical aptitude also paled in comparison to that of an elf.

Despite this, humans stood at the pinnacle of the Alliance of Four Races.

Why, you ask?

Because they were smarter than the elves. They valued wisdom and knowledge above all else and were good at collecting information. The human ability to collect information is formidable, and it has enabled them to overcome their other shortcomings on more occasions than it is possible to count.

Both Houston the Pig Slayer and Breeze Kugel, aka the Strangler, had provided Bash with great information in the past.

Yes, human information was precious and valuable.

And...the Great Merchant Bly.

The name Great Merchant didn't mean much to Bash, but most knew him by the moniker Paper Mage Bly.

He would obtain key information about the enemy forces from goodness knows where and identify ambush locations on a war map.

The result was victory.

And although Bash did not know of this, the demon warlord was often heard to lament, "I've been outsmarted by that damn Bly once again."

Although he never appeared on the front line, he was the top man among a race that was generally amazing at handling information.

So that was Bly.

Of all members of the Coalition of Seven, only the Demon Lord Geddigs had ever surpassed him.

However, it was Bly who sent a death squad, including the Human Prince Nazar, to fight Geddigs.

Now in peacetime, Bly was using his skills to supply other kinds of information sought by the people. Magazine specials on love and marriage were hot sellers. That was the tide of the times, you see.

"Speaking of Bly, he's the man who wrested victory from us with a perfect strategy, eh, Boss?"

"So then, if I follow the information in this magazine written by Bly..."

"You'll be able to find a wife in no time flat!"

Bash stooped and took the magazine from Zell.

His hands trembled as he lifted it up, like a mage who's just stumbled upon a great tome of the forbidden magical arts.

A magazine. A special issue on love and marriage. The beastkin's cultural views on romance and dating.

What else could have been more perfect for Bash's current situation?

Bash wasn't above asking around to find out more about folk, but the beastkin probably weren't expecting to get questions of that sort in this day and age. So he'd probably have some trouble finding someone who could tell him in depth about what he needed to know.

But now he had all the information he could need in his very hands.

(Although up until this point, he'd been sure victory was secure right up until the moment he realized it was a lost cause...)

Bash had seen many battles.

When he was a new recruit, he'd had no idea what was going on with the war in general.

But as he gained experience, he gradually figured out how to tell which side was superior and which side was inferior.

Of course, just knowing the trend of the battle wasn't enough to be able to accurately predict who'd win, but...nevertheless, Bash had learned to identify the specific situations in which the flow of battle changed.

At the end of the war, there were times when he had an inkling about who would win before the battle even began.

That was exactly how he felt right now.

"I feel almost moved to tears! So much has happened, but the day when you tie the knot is right around the corner now, don'cha think, Boss?"

Zell was swept up in the emotion of the moment, too.

"Indeed."

Bash laughed.

After leaving the country of orcs, he had visited the countries of the humans, elves, and dwarves.

Now he stood in the Red Forest. Thinking back on it, he had come a long way...

"However, I can't let my guard down and just go assuming I'll be victorious. I must remain vigilant."

"That's right! No matter how good your tactics are, if you lose focus, you can easily end up losing the whole battle!"

"Precisely."

"Anyway, I wonder why this magazine was thrown away here, in a place like this. And a human magazine, at that..."

A discarded magazine doesn't mean much of anything. People tend to toss them away when they're done reading them.

But this pair didn't see it that way.

They couldn't imagine throwing away something so precious for no reason.

And they'd have found it hard to believe that one can purchase a magazine for about the cost of an hour of labor.

"...Could it have been...that man from before?"

"Ah, that's right! I'll bet that's right, Boss! He was a human, so it wouldn't be strange for him to have a human magazine!"

The pair thought back to the man they'd met near the border.

Errol, the emissary of love and peace. He was a man with a mysterious atmosphere. Perhaps he'd overheard Bash and Zell conversing and deliberately dropped the magazine.

Because he was the emissary of *love* and peace, see.

"The next time we meet, I'll have to say thank you."

"Right, Boss!"

They'd thank him not only for helping them at the border but also for the magazine.

But the man would no doubt be confused. Because it wasn't he who'd dropped the magazine.

"Well, what does it say?"

"Hmm, let's see... 'Beastkin Love and Marriage Values No One Tells You About These Days'... 'Cool Outfit Choices for Marriage Seekers'... Ooh, this is some amazing information! Finding a beastkin bride is going to be easier than taking candy from a baby!"

"You think so?"

The two were extremely excited over having stumbled upon a treasure trove of information... And they hadn't even got to town yet!

The magazine was bursting with exactly the information Bash wanted.

"Well, first of all, the current trends among beastkin women are..."

"Hmm..."

The two of them pored over the magazine.

Their expressions were extremely serious. And if someone stumbled upon them like that, they'd have looked for all the world like strategists at a military council, thinking about a plan to overturn a desperate situation.

With the magazine in hand, the future was bright for Bash.

■　　■　　■

The capital of the beastkin country, Lycant.

Although it was called the capital, it was a relatively new town.

After the war, it took a year to dismantle the long-established fortress and rebuild it into a place where people could live. It had been two years since people moved in and started living their lives. Everything was brand-new, and clean, and tidy, but it still felt oddly empty.

But the beastkin were eager to live there. The beastkin equivalent of the royal family set up their residence first, and they were followed by the beastkin equivalent of the aristocracy.

Then came the commonfolk, the ones who had lost their homes; the middle classes, who worshipped the aristocracy and the royalty; and then finally the lower classes.

The high beastkin folk who remained in the Green Forest nonetheless supported those who decided to live in Lycant.

And why did they seek so much to live here?

Because this place was sacred to them.

It was the birthplace of their spiritual religion, Licantism, and the land where the Sacred Tree grew.

It was a special place for the beastkin tribe.

And because it was that kind of town, they were relatively tolerant of outsiders.

Yes, it was a sacred place, but it was also where the beastkin tribe was united, and they all burned with passion to restore the town.

You might say the wedding of the third-born princess, Innuella, was also part of that.

Three years after the war, Lycant, the capital, had become a splendid town. It became a place truly worthy of being called a sacred place for the beastkin tribe.

And the ceremony was to serve as a sort of unveiling of the new town. Kings and aristocrats of various races were invited, and it was widely advertised to the general public of each country. On the occasion of the marriage of the third princess, free lodging would be provided for those without a roof, free food for those who were hungry, and jobs for those without paid work.

As long as the visitors joined the celebration.

A festival, of sorts.

And so, while the guards defending Lycant were wary of any trouble being caused in the town, they were quite tolerant of visitors.

Not only humans, elves, and dwarves, but also lizardmen, harpies, fairies, and even succubi and demons were invited into the town, unconditionally.

All were welcome…except orcs.

"Oh…"

A soldier standing at the entrance of the town gasped when he saw a creature with green skin and long fangs among the crowd who were coming in from the road.

But he could say nothing.

Because the orc was impeccably dressed.

He wore the same kind of open kimono that residents of the beastkin country often wore. The material was not cloth but fur, probably from an Aoshima wolf, but it looked surprisingly nice against his green skin.

He also wore a belt of bark from the Kuten tree around his waist, a sword on his back wrapped in the fur of the scaly rabbit, and shoes woven from the vines of the big-eater plant on his feet.

And that wasn't all. It was faint, but the orc had a floral scent about him. He didn't have that fishy musk peculiar to orcs. *This* orc had clearly bathed and applied cologne.

He was dressed perfectly in the formal attire of the beastkin tribe.

The beastkin usually wear clothes made from materials such as linen and cotton, but during important ceremonies, they cover their entire bodies with animal products in gratitude to the god of the hunt.

"Oh, oh, oh…"

The soldier was at a loss for words.

No orcs allowed! In the name of the former Dog Corps!

It was a feeling shared among the soldiers, although it was not spoken of publicly.

But had there ever been an orc so impeccably dressed?

Had the orcs ever been so attuned to the culture of the beastkin tribe?

No. On the contrary, even the humans and the elves didn't bother themselves with dressing in beastkin formal attire.

Not that it was much of an issue.

No, it was not much of an issue. But the beastkin tribe would certainly have smiled to see representatives from each country embracing the beastkin culture.

And this orc was doing precisely that.

Based on his attire, he had come all the way from the orc country specifically to participate in the beastkin ceremony.

He had even taken into consideration the overly sensitive noses of the beastkin tribe and had applied cologne.

"I'd like to pass, please?"

"Oh! Certainly!"

As a soldier of the town gate, he was prepared to turn away all orcs, even if it cost him his life.

But this orc had come in such perfect attire and had shown such cultural consideration... So the guard could do nothing, say nothing against him. He had no choice but to stand aside and watch as the orc passed through...

3
Amazing Atmosphere! Big Crowds and Taverns!

The capital, Lycant, was overflowing with people, perhaps because it was right before the wedding of the third-born princess.

Various races were present, but the most common were the resident beastkin.

The beastkin race has a lot of variety to it, compared to other races.

Some look like wild beasts walking upright, and some look exactly like humans, just with animal ears.

Many had beastlike characteristics. Some were doglike, some catlike, some rabbitlike; some had deerlike horns, some had bearlike physiques, and some had a combination of these features...

Beastkin ideas of beauty were based on things like nose size, eyelash length, and hair style. But from an outsider's perspective, they all looked like a real mishmash.

It was said that these characteristics did not exist in the early days of the war.

At that time, everyone resembled something more akin to a wild beast.

However, as the war intensified, the beastkin began to mingle with other races such as humans, elves, and dwarves.

As a result, the old beastkin features were slowly bred out.

A large figure moved through the beastkin crowd.

The eyes of passersby widened when they looked upon the figure, and they turned around to continue watching him as he passed.

"But you know, Boss, there seems to be so many different kinds of beastkin."

"Indeed."

The figure was Bash.

He'd dressed exactly as the magazine recommended and was now taking a stroll around town.

Bash thought he had the perfect outfit.

Taking action based on reliable information was a tactic Bash had utilized many times during wartime.

Subtle, meticulous actions were the style, especially when the Demon Lord Geddigs was still alive.

Act according to strategy, and victory will be assured. Make even the slightest mistake in strategy, or act sloppily, and defeat will be the result.

But after Geddigs's death... Or perhaps it was around the time of the final battle of the Remium Plateau... Bash himself had grown so strong that there was little need for meticulous planning, but he still knew the value of perfect execution.

So he did everything the magazine said.

The magazine had an article on "Attire Ladies Love!" which Bash had studied, and then his plan was to run around the Red Forest hunting beasts to gather the requisite raw materials. But by complete chance, he'd happened upon a traveling merchant who was being attacked by magical beasts. The merchant was so grateful to Bash for saving his life that he'd presented to Bash the exact same clothes as the ones shown in the magazine. And when the merchant saw the clothes didn't fit, he had spent the whole night retailoring them.

Therefore, the clothes were perfect.

"What kind of young lady would you like for your wife, Boss? One that's not too *beastly*, I imagine?"

"I'm not feeling very picky."

Beastkin weren't particularly Bash's type.

It didn't matter if she looked like a human or an elf, or a dog or cat, as long as she was a woman. If Bash had to exercise a veto, it would probably be for lizardfolk and dwarves, as neither race's women *typically* lit a fire in his belly and elsewhere.

"But I'd still prefer someone close in appearance to a human or elf."

Bash couldn't stop himself from adding this one caveat.

He thought back on Judith, whom he'd met in Krassel; Thunder Sonia, whom he'd met in the Shiwanashi Forest; and Primera, whom he'd met in Dobanga Pit.

They had all been exceptionally beautiful to Bash.

Even now, he'd be happy to marry all three of them and have five children with each.

You could say they were the ones who got away.

"That's right, Boss! If you ask me, beastly beastkin are no better than…beasts! Their breath stinks, and all they do is try to eat me! Hey! Did you see that one over there? It practically started drooling as soon as it saw me!"

When Bash looked where Zell was pointing, he found that there was indeed a beastkin who was drooling.

But their gaze went right through Zell to focus instead on a store selling grilled meat.

"Well, I'm not the one who has to marry one of them, so what do I care? Now then, Boss. Our first objective, just like the magazine said, should be to head to a bar with the right kind of vibes!"

"Right!"

Their destination was the most popular bar in Lycant.

And why were they heading to such a place? It was all down to an article written in that magazine.

It said:

Good Vibes! Head to a place where many people gather and the drinks flow freely! Top Best Nightlife Venues:

It appeared that beastkin women preferred to be seduced in a group, rather than being approached alone.

Therefore, after Bash entered Lycant and secured lodgings at an inn, he immediately headed out to the *battlefield*.

Yes, the most bustling watering hole in Lycant, just as the magazine said!

"…Hmm?"

"Hmm? What's that sound?"

Their ears rang with an unpleasant noise.

A cacophony, somewhere between the death squeal of a pig and a butchered cow's bellow.

An ominous sort of noise, the kind of noise that heralded the coming of something unpleasant…

"Heeeyyy, baaaabe! ♪ Whooo! Yeah! Ladidadida! ♪ Everybodyyy! ♪ Peeeace and looove... ♪"

And on top of that...horrible, horrible singing.

Passersby covered their ears, scowled, and scurried past the man.

"Isn't that Mr. Errol over there, Boss?"

It was Bash's ministering angel.

Errol, the emissary of love and peace, who'd helped them out at the border and left that magazine for Bash.

He sat by the side of the road, clearly enjoying the sound of his own singing.

"Errol!"

When Bash called out to him, he looked up, and his eyes widened.

"Oh? Oh!"

He immediately stood up, came to Bash, and stared at him from head to toe.

"If it isn't Lord Bash! Why, I didn't see you there!"

Because he was wearing a mask, his expression wasn't visible, but his voice was filled with surprise and joy.

It was the sound of a man surprised by a great trick, one performed by someone he hadn't been expecting anything of.

"Ah, you know, I thought you were a bit late getting to town! But you were procuring yourself some clothes, weren't you? I'd expect no less of the Orc Hero! You're so thoughtful, you know, one could scarcely believe you're an orc! Indeed, this surpasses all expectations!"

"Thank you. Thank you for your assistance."

"At the border, you mean? Well now, don't mention that! But come! Let me show you around!"

Errol happily took Bash's hand and pulled him along.

"Wait, where are you going?"

"Where...?"

"I have a destination in mind already."

"A destination, you say?"

"Yes. It's a well-populated place where you can drink alcohol."

When Bash said that, Errol looked taken aback for a moment, but then he laughed as if what Bash said had made perfect sense.

"Ha-ha-ha. That's a funny way of saying it. But it's okay, we're going to the same destination!"

"Is that so?"

"So you came for a bit of that, too, eh?"

How did this man know Bash's intended destination? ...It was Zell who zoomed close to Bash's ear to clear that question up.

(Boss, if you really think about it, he's the one who left us that magazine, so of course he can guess where you're going!)

(Hmm, is that true?)

(Actually, there's a possibility that he'll take you somewhere even *better* than the bar written about in the magazine.)

(I see!)

Convinced by Zell's explanation, Bash turned to Errol.

"All right then, will you be our guide?"

"Leave it to me!"

Errol led Bash deeper into the heart of the capital.

■　■　■

Bash found himself in the courtyard of a huge palace, right in the center of Lycant.

It was the most glittering and luxurious space Bash had ever seen.

Large tables had been brought into the palace's courtyard garden, and a mountain of food was prepared. The people were dressed in colorful costumes of fine cloth that were adorned with gold and silver jewelry.

Just looking at it all made Bash's eyes swim.

Errol escorted Bash in and said, "I'm going to do a quick lap and schmooze. Please take it easy, relax, and eat your fill of the food." Then he was gone.

Bash and Zell were left alone.

"What are you going to do, Boss? This isn't the place you had in mind, is it?"

"...It isn't, but this place isn't bad."

It wasn't the place that was written about in the magazine. It wasn't even a bar.

However, there were a lot of people, and apparently the alcohol was all-you-can-drink.

"Then there's only one thing to do."

It was the same as on the battlefield.

While traveling, there were many times when Bash was taken to a different location than the battlefield he'd heard about in advance.

There were many times when he was thrown into a situation that was different from what he'd expected.

Bash had survived every single one of those surprise scenarios.

So he figured...even if the destination was different than he'd expected, as long as his mission was unchanged, he would not waver.

"What did the magazine say you should do when you come to the bar, again?"

"Drink fruity red wine at a nice bar, adopt a casual lean, and wait to be approached by a woman... That's the winning strategy the magazine mentioned, Boss!"

"I see."

Bash surveyed his surroundings restlessly, saw the booze he was looking for on one of the tables, and reached for it.

Fruity wine in a delicate glass.

For someone of Bash's stature, the glass only contained around one to two sips of wine, but getting drunk wasn't his objective anyway.

Bash held the glass in his meaty hand and parked himself in a corner, leaning as casually as he could.

With his excellent core strength, the tilted glass remained steady in his hand, as if a slight angle was how it was always meant to be held, according to all laws of physics.

Of course, he did not bring the glass to his lips.

The magazine never said anything about actually *drinking* the booze.

"Still, this is pretty fancy, huh, Boss? I've slipped into human parties once or twice, but this is the first time I've been anywhere this fancy! I heard rumors that the beastkin were flat broke, but... Well, they sure know how to flex! Or maybe they're broke because they spent all their money on this party...?"

"Could be."

"Well, money's not important! Let's focus on finding you a lady!"

Bash and Zell took another look around.

There were many different races, but beastkin and elves were especially common. There were quite a few humans in attendance as well, but not as many dwarves. They all glanced at Bash with quizzical looks on their faces.

Those looks seemed to say, *Hey, is it all right for an orc to be here?*

"Hmm. You know, Boss, seems there's quite a lot of noble types here."

"Oh?"

"Their clothes are all sparkly."

From where Bash was standing, it seemed most of the beastkin men wore clothes similar to the ones Bash was wearing.

However, many of the beastkin women, elves, and humans wore bulky ornaments over their cotton and silk kimonos.

Bash, of course, didn't care much about fashion.

This was a party, and men and women were happily chatting. On closer inspection, though, Bash noticed groups of men surrounding the women with lustful smiles. The women smiled back at them, looking pleased by the attention. And the clothing the women wore was skimpy, exposing ample cleavage and thighs.

The men's eyes—those of the human men in particular—were practically glued to the women's chests. Bash's eyes went naturally to their cleavage as well, and he snorted air through his nose.

"There's so many of them, it's intimidating."

There wasn't a single unattractive beastkin woman there.

The fact that they were all wearing low-cut tops may have skewed Bash's judgment, though.

With so much skin on display, how could they fail to draw looks of desire?

"No, no, Boss. Right now, you've got to stand firm and wait. You're no rookie soldier, and if you ignore the standby order and rush in, the name of the Orc Hero will be besmirched!"

"I know that."

It was important, this time, to try not to strike up conversation with anyone.

The magazine clearly said to wait patiently. So Bash would wait.

Bash didn't quite get it, but actually, there was a good reason for that.

The beastkin country was a matriarchal society. The ruler was a woman, and women often held the most important posts. In their culture and history, women had been the leaders of the pack ever since ancient times. The beastkin also heavily subscribed to polygamy.

It was a very different standard from that of humans.

One major cultural difference was in how men "approached" women.

To prove their strength, they would hunt outside town, clothe themselves with the materials they'd gathered, and then wait for a woman to come and talk to them.

During the war, many wore the fangs of slain orcs and the horns of demons.

It was said that a beastkin woman who married more—and stronger—men would rise in the ranks as a pack leader.

"Doesn't look like anyone's coming to chat with you, huh, Boss?"

"You're too restless, Zell. These things take time."

"Hmm... That's all well and good, but I'm a fairy, y'know? I'm not good at sitting still. If I go too long without moving, my instincts will start whispering to me. *Fly! Fly,* they'll say! *What do you think these wings are for? They're for flying! For zooming!* Why, back in Centaur Valley, I..."

Zell was about to launch into one of their tales of heroism, back before Bash's warrior days had even begun, when—

"Yeeeeeeek!!!!!"

—there came a scream.

"Wh-wh-what's happening?!" Zell yelped and looked all around in confusion.

The gazes of all nearby were focused on Zell.

Ah, of course. Zell was a superstar of the fairy world. At one mention of their fairy bravery, the fangirls and boys had come swarming.

"An *orc*!"

Whoops. Scratch that.

One of the beastkin women, dressed in a silk kimono and a tiger pelt, was pointing at Bash.

Now everyone was looking at him.

Bash was a superstar in the orc world, so perhaps it was par for the course...

"What's an *orc* doing here?!"

"Hey! That orc's here to assault the women!"

"Guards! Where are the guards?!"

"Throw it out! No, beat it up!"

The screams of the women had the place in pandemonium within seconds.

Some fled from Bash, some yelled for the guards, and some rolled up their sleeves and advanced upon him menacingly.

All things considered, even Bash could understand he was not welcome.

"Wait, please! This man is the strongest orc alive! He dominated in countless battles during the last war, and among the orc folk, he has been given the lauded title of Orc Hero! What's more, he was brought here, you know?! By that guy who wears the mask... Ero... Erik...or something like that!"

Zell tried to defend Bash, but no one listened.

Bash was gradually surrounded. And to add insult to injury, he was surrounded by *men*.

"Pipe down! What's the meaning of this?"

Then came a voice from the back of the hall.

Bash turned to see three beauties in a league of their own—the type to make one gulp upon seeing them.

Each had different degrees of beastlike blood in her, but they all had heaving breasts and plump thighs, and they wore the most colorful clothes of anyone in the room. When they saw Bash, they froze.

"Look... The princesses..."

"For some reason, there appears to be an orc here."

"Don't worry, I shall dispose of him right now."

Princess. Hearing that title brought up a word from Bash's memory.

The six beastkin princesses. Yes, six beautiful princesses born to the Beastkin Queen. Rumor had it that all six of them were peerless beauties, strong and clever...

"...Beautiful..."

Yes, and the three women before him were beautiful beyond Bash's imagination.

One princess had a coat like a black cat's fur, golden eyes, and a supple body.

Another full-bodied princess had fluffy fur and black eyes.

And the third princess had somewhat coarse fur, blue eyes, and a sturdy body like that of a hunting dog.

Three princesses. Despite being sisters, they all appeared to be different breeds of beastkin. Still, there was no denying that all of them were knockouts. They were as beautiful as the rumors suggested, if not more so.

However, the three paid no attention to the gossip.

Staring at Bash, their eyes widened.

The soft smiles had faded from each of their faces, and their pupils had contracted.

"You are…"

The moment one of the three muttered his name, all the clamoring crowd fell silent.

The beastkin among the crowd were especially silent and still.

The elves and humans, though confused and perplexed, had not been kicking up such a fuss as the beastkin to begin with.

And then, as confusion subsided, another emotion swirled in the eyes of the beastkin.

Everyone turned their gazes to Bash.

Such hateful, evil gazes.

"There are many people who don't know his face, but there are none who do not know his name."

The princesses stepped forward in front of Bash.

At the same time, the strong men who seemed to be their escorts also stepped forward to protect them.

The men wore expressions of hatred on their faces.

At the same time, the fear of death was in their eyes. It was as if, on some level, they realized they were picking a fight with someone only a fool with a death wish would challenge.

"Orc Hero Bash! You are the one who killed our uncle, the beastkin brave, Leto!"

◆　◆　◆

The beastkin brave, Leto.

He was a Hero who had died honorably in battle against the Demon Lord Geddigs on the Remium Plateau.

That's what the legends said, but the truth was a little different.

Indeed, the brave Leto fought the Demon Lord Geddigs.

The Human Prince Nazar. The Elf Archmage Thunder Sonia.

The Beastkin Hero Leto. The Dwarf Battlelord Doradoradobanga.

Along with a dozen others, he infiltrated deep into the enemy's camp, fought the Demon Lord, and defeated him.

The sacrifice was great. Almost all members of the suicide squad were killed in action, including the Battlelord Doradoradobanga.

But Leto was still alive when Geddigs died.

Despite being covered in wounds, he had survived. If anything, he was in better shape than Thunder Sonia, who had run out of magic and fainted.

But then *he* appeared.

A lone orc.

At the time, the green devil was the talk of the battlefield.

Later, he would be titled the Orc Hero Bash.

Nazar and Leto tried to fight against this orc.

But they were simply no match for Bash. No matter how brave the beastkin were or how brave the human prince was, they had no hope of victory. As they were badly wounded already, the fight shifted in Bash's favor almost immediately.

If Thunder Sonia had still been conscious, or if Doradoradobanga was still alive, things might have gone differently. However, Nazar was injured, and Leto's remaining physical strength was at its limit.

Moreover, the fight took place in the middle of the enemy's camp, and both knew that if the battle was prolonged, another enemy would surely spring up.

So Leto the Brave spoke.

"Leave this to me and go."

Nazar obeyed.

Someone had to make it back alive.

Someone had to tell everyone that Geddigs had been defeated. Otherwise, his death could have been covered up, and only the news that the finest men of the Alliance of Four had been killed in action would be spread.

If that happened, the fighting spirit of the Alliance of Four would crumble, and the war situation would worsen. They would be overwhelmed in an instant. By the time the news of Geddigs's death spread, it would have been too late, and all four races would have been wiped out.

That had to be avoided at all cost.

Nazar carried Thunder Sonia on his back, broke through enemy lines, and completed his report.

As a result, the Alliance of Four won the decisive battle of the Remium Plateau.

And later on...Leto's corpse was found on the battlefield.

The corpse was in a pitiful state. The weapon had been smashed, and the torso had been completely split in half.

Leto the Brave.

Leto Rivergold. The younger brother of the royal beastkin Rivergold family.

A man who was loved and respected by all the members of the royal family...

His name should have struck fear into the hearts of his every enemy across every continent, but his head hadn't even been recovered from his corpse.

Beastkin saw no shame in defeat.

Being brought low by a mighty foe was said to bring honor upon a person's name. The beastkin followed the doctrine of the god of the hunt; they fed on the prey they slew themselves. Thus, they also found honor in being defeated by their prey should they be bested in battle. In such a scenario, they would willingly submit to being devoured themselves.

It had been thousands of years since beastkin ceased the practice of eating people, but other facets of the doctrine remained. They found no shame in being defeated in battle or having their heads taken as trophies.

Rather, beastkin were proud to die valiantly and would be glad to have news of their honorable defeat spread.

But Leto had received no such treatment.

The enemy did not celebrate Leto's defeat as the beastkin might have hoped. In death, he was treated as a common soldier.

The Hero, a man who should have been honored by the one to defeat him, had been left to rot.

And so the beastkin royal family resented Bash.

They despised him for making light of Leto's death.

From that day on, Bash had become their sworn enemy.

And so all beastkin knew the name of Bash.

Especially the warriors who'd survived the battle of the Remium Plateau.

Now this mortal enemy had appeared, and the place was in an uproar.

The princesses were outraged and made no attempt to hide it.

"What brings you here, Orc *Hero*?!"

"...I heard the third-born princess was getting married."

"So you decided to show up and attack our sister Innuella! You! Our mortal enemy!"

"That wasn't my intention..."

"You fool! Do you think we will forgive your tyranny?! I'll flay the skin of your corpse and reclaim the beastkin honor!"

As she spoke, one princess drew her sword from her bosom.

"That's right! It's our good luck that he showed up here!"

"Even if we know we cannot win, if we do not take revenge on our enemies, then who will avenge us?!"

The other two also followed suit.

In an instant, Bash was surrounded by three beautiful women. But not in the way he might have fantasized about.

The fairy flitted about among the four of them.

"H-hey, wait a minute! It's true that the boss killed Leto, but that battlefield was in total chaos, so what do you expect?! A lot of things like that happened on the battlefield. It's common knowledge! Even the boss and I passed out, and when we woke up, it was so bad that we thought we were in another world. So many of our comrades, slain..."

"Who cares?!"

The princesses would not be swayed.

They had their swords ready at their hips, preparing to attack Bash.

"I don't want to fight, but..."

Bash wasn't really sure what was going on, but he had no intention of killing such beautiful women.

However, if beastkin attacked him with honor and pride, then Bash was duty bound to fight back and to win for the honor and pride of the orcs.

Bash raised his hand to the hilt of his sword.

"B-Boss?! Are you serious?! If you kill the beastkin princesses, there will be another war, you know?!"

"I know, but it's true that I killed the Hero Leto."

"But......"

It happened in an instant.

Some of the onlookers stiffened as they watched everything unfold.

The war was over. Everyone was trying to forget the grudges of the war and move forward. The marriage of the beastkin princess and the elf soldier was supposed to be part of that.

So then, why were the Orc Hero and the beastkin princesses trying to start a fight in a place like this?

In the unlikely event that someone died, would it not only result in another war?

The Orc Hero seemed reluctant.

And on closer inspection, the princesses' bodyguards and the other beastkin surrounding the Orc Hero looked rather panicked. They dripped with cold sweat, and their eyes were rolling around in their sockets as if to say, *Are we really doing this?*

Only the princesses were serious.

They wore their murderous intent openly and seemed ready to cut Bash down at a moment's notice.

"...!"

The princesses' boots scraped against the ground as they dropped into fighting stances.

           *   *   *

"Hello, everyone. What seems to be the problem?"

A clear voice, like the ringing of a bell, resounded.

"...This is supposed to be a joyous occasion. We're gathered here today to celebrate Innuella's wedding, so why do you all seem so intent on having a funeral?"

Bash lifted his head and gulped.

How...exquisite...

Another beautiful girl.

She was a touch petite but large in the chest, with a narrow waist and hips that any man would long to grab.

Her countenance was moderately human...elven, even.

She had a slender face with narrow eyes and a small mouth, and vulpine ears were atop her head.

She exuded the purity of a crystal-clear stream.

"Silviana... So you're here. It is an auspicious day, yes, and yet this interloper..."

"Go on..."

"...He's the man who killed the great Leto..."

"Hmm? Ah! So this is him, huh? The Orc Hero Bash?"

Silviana.

The girl who answered to that name brought a hand to her mouth and looked at Bash in confusion.

Then she frowned and spoke in solemn tones.

"But, Sisters, the war is over. It's true that we've lived with hatred for the orcs and those who humiliated Uncle Leto. But look around you. We are restoring our holy land, and Innuella is to be married. This is an era of peace."

"I can't believe you just said that..."

"Lord Bash also came all the way here to celebrate Innuella's marriage and the glory of the beastkin race, so shouldn't we also forgive him and accept him with generous hearts?"

"How can you say that?!"

"Look at his attire."

Everyone took another look at Bash's clothing.

Indeed, his manner of dress was most unusual for an orc.

Wearing the formal attire of the beastkin tribe, he held a glass of wine at a tilt.

It was plain to see that the contents of the glass were full; he likely hadn't had a single sip.

Many orcs acted violently when inebriated, so clearly, this one was restraining himself.

Yes, that much was plain to see.

He had come here only to celebrate the marriage of the third-born beastkin princess.

"Or are we, the beastkin royal family, so narrow-minded that we wouldn't even allow that?"

The other princesses were taken aback by Silviana's words.

Silviana chuckled.

"Furthermore..."

She narrowed her eyes and looked up at Bash.

Then she approached him as he stood there in confusion, still not entirely sure what was going on.

"...When I heard about the orc who killed Uncle Leto, I imagined him to be uglier, but isn't this man rather masculine and sincere-looking?"

Then she put her hand on Bash's strong arm, gently snuggled up, and said:

"I think I just fell in love!"

And just like that, spring had finally come for Bash.

4
The Top Bar in the Capital, Lycant

Several hours had passed since the mayhem at the party venue.

"… *This man is my love. Please let him go free.*"

With those words from the princess called Silviana, the dispute was settled.

However, Bash was still hated by the beastkin royal family, and he was forced to leave.

As he learned on his way out, the party was being held at the royal palace, Lycaon. It seemed to be where the third-born princess's wedding reception was to be held.

Aristocrats and royalty from all over the world would gather there to feast for several days.

Why did Errol take Bash there, and how was Bash granted admittance anyway?

After all, no one had questioned him over Bash's presence in the slightest.

The answer was really quite simple. No one knew that Errol had escorted Bash and Zell to the event.

That detail was lost on Bash and Zell, since orcs and fairies weren't the type to pay attention to trifling details.

Bash was simply grateful and rather moved.

He had dressed as instructed by the magazine, gone to a popular venue as described in the magazine, and had caught the attention of a beautiful woman, just as the magazine said he would.

Silviana Rivergold, the fifth-born princess of the beastin country.

She was a gorgeous woman with a mostly human appearance who had declared that she'd fallen in love with Bash at first sight. She'd had herself so tightly wrapped around his arm that he could feel her voluptuous breasts pressing into him.

When she saw Bash off at the exit of the venue, she'd put her mouth to Bash's ear, and with a voice that made him melt, whispered:

"Let's meet again."

And then she kissed Bash on the cheek.

That had been more than enough to give Bash hope.

This peerless beastkin beauty wanted a romantic relationship with him.

The thought of this was enough to make Bash's soldier stand at attention, eager for a chance to be called into action.

It wouldn't be an exaggeration to say that a countdown had begun... Every second he would be made to wait until the glorious day he bedded his beautiful beastkin bride would feel like an eternity.

In his long search for a wife, had he ever had such a smooth encounter?

In a word, no.

However promising his prospects seemed, things had ultimately ended poorly with the humans, the elves, and the dwarves.

This change in fortune was all thanks to Errol, who'd provided the magazine and brought Bash there.

To be fair, there was some unpleasantness, but the results were what truly mattered. All else was trivial.

"I owe Errol my thanks."

"That's right! I can't believe how easily you snagged that beastkin princess..."

Bash was now at the bar he had originally planned to visit.

They were there drinking in celebration of the day's success.

"I truly can't thank him enough. I'd heard humans were good at collecting information and strategizing, but I didn't think they were *this* good."

"I, for my part, may have misunderstood the human race. I figured the only thing special about them was the fact that they were a little brainy, but who knew they'd go so far to help a complete stranger?"

They both praised Errol.

In their eyes, Errol was heaven-sent. They were ready to worship at the altar of Errol.

At the bar, there were several beastkin men dressed similarly to Bash.

All were drinking fruity red wine.

It was almost as if a glass of fruit wine in hand was some universal sign of availability.

In fact, some beastkin men were sitting next to beastkin women and engaging in spirited conversation.

Some had been doing that when Bash entered, and some of the women had approached some of the men while Bash was drinking alone.

The magazine article had been spot-on.

But Bash wasn't here to hunt girls.

After all, he'd already been claimed by a beastkin princess just earlier. The beastkin right of polygamy was limited to women. Polyandry, to be more precise. And it was considered unfaithful for a man to approach multiple women.

Just like with the elves, it would be best to narrow his attentions down to one woman.

Bash hadn't even considered what it would be like to be but one of a woman's multiple lovers. He hadn't spared a single thought for how that might mar his orcish pride.

"She said you'd meet again, Boss, but when?"

"Soon, no doubt."

Orcs had no need for things like subterfuge or trickery, and so they had little experience with said tactics.

Of course, they knew nothing of social etiquette, either.

Therefore, Bash took the words *Let's meet again* at face value.

"Still, Boss, you can't let your guard down and start slacking now. Just like the magazine said, you have to be careful!"

"I know. When I get back to the inn, I'll review the magazine again."

"Good idea, Boss!"

The magazine also described what would happen if you actually ended up dating someone.

It carefully described the process of mating and all the techniques that would make a man a hit with a beastkin woman.

Bash intended to follow the instructions to the letter.

There could be no mistake in what was written in that magazine.

Bash tilted his glass of fruit wine.

He swirled it around in the glass, smelled it, and sipped it.

It wasn't how an orc usually treated booze, but according to the magazine, this technique was sure to please, so Bash was determined to practice it.

Some time passed after that.

It was peaceful. No one tried to talk to Bash, and Bash kept to himself as well. Zell and Bash leisurely sipped their drinks while reminiscing.

It was possible that some of the beastkin warriors had overheard Bash and Zell's conversation and wanted to approach them. But it was decided that this was a bar for meeting ladies. It was not a place for men to talk to men, so Bash refrained.

"Oh?"

Bash heard a voice from behind him. It came just as a drunken Zell, having glugged three glasses of fruit wine, was about to stage a duel against a dish of peanuts over the favor of a pretty lady's hand (the "lady" being a dish of almonds).

"...?"

When Bash turned around, he met eyes with another beautiful woman.

Wait, *was* she a beauty? It was hard to tell. She was dressed in a rugged, baggy dark-brown robe, with a hood and a mask pulled over her eyes to hide her face.

Bash could only see her eyes.

But they were soft eyes that would bewitch any who looked upon them. The figure had thin, well-shaped eyebrows, and what little skin Bash could see was porcelain white and free of imperfection.

Her mouth was covered by a mask, and her hair was tucked into her hood.

From the vague outline of her cloak, Bash could guess she was probably rather curvy beneath it, but he couldn't be sure.

Every other man in the bar seemed more than sure, however.

Not only were the single men waiting to be hit on, but even the men who were already chatting with women were marveling at her and likely thinking to themselves:

Now there's *a woman without equal!*

The whole place filled with the sound of rustling and fidgeting. This way and that,

men could be seen fixing their hair, straightening their postures, and adjusting their sitting positions so that they could appear as desirable as possible.

Some even seemed to be debating whether to leave their seats and go over to her.

"It's rare to see an orc in this country..."

She had a sultry voice. It was pure velvet.

Hers was a voice that was dripping with sex appeal yet altogether different from Silviana's captivating tone.

But like Silviana, this new woman's voice had the power to make Bash's heart crash against his ribcage.

And the owner of the voice was speaking directly to him.

"I've seen you somewhere before... You... No, could it be...?"

The shrouded woman looked at Bash and then, with a spring in her step, hurried over to him.

"You're... You're the Orc Hero Bash, aren't you?"

"...Erm, yes, that's right."

Bash remembered her the moment he heard her voice.

"It's me!"

"...Ah."

"Do you, um, remember me...?"

The beauty frowned.

Well, it can't be helped, I suppose… After all, from his point of view, I'm lower than garbage… That was the sort of statement behind the sadness in her eyes.

"I remember you. You're Carrot. Carrot the Breathstealer, they called you."

"Y-yes! Oh, I'm so happy! You really do remember me!"

The beautiful woman, Carrot, smiled like a flower in bloom.

She looked happy. Truly elated. As she smiled, her immaculate eyes creased until they all but disappeared beneath her mask.

With a smile like that, she'd open herself up to all sorts of misunderstandings.

But Bash remained steadfast.

"What a surprise! I certainly didn't expect to run into you here of all places."

"I could say the same. I didn't know you'd be here."

Bash took a sidelong glance at Carrot as he spoke.

A sharp black tail peeked out from the hem of her robes.

And on closer inspection, parts of her hood were also unnaturally raised. Almost as if it had corners.

"Aren't succubi forbidden from leaving the country?"

"Not exactly... When in other countries, we're prohibited from showing our skin and hair and such, but that doesn't mean we can't leave the country *at all*..."

Carrot...

She was a succubus. The traditional clothing of the succubi was naturally skimpy and exposed a lot of skin.

In some cases, they walked around with certain body parts entirely exposed. Other countries would consider walking around with those same body parts exposed the height of indecency.

But Carrot was covered from head to toe.

"I never thought we would meet again, Sir Bash. And certainly not in a place like this... Why would someone as magnificent as yourself be...? Oh, excuse me. Now that I notice your attire, the reasoning seems perfectly clear."

"..."

"Oh, don't give me that look. We're more alike than you think..."

Then Carrot narrowed her eyes.

She was smiling, presumably. With her face mostly hidden, the only part of her Bash could see was those narrowed eyes.

However, just from that look, he could sense that her succubus pheromones were already hard at work. He could almost smell them.

"It's a shame I'm not the one you have your sights set on, but how about we have a drink together anyway?"

"I would never turn down a drink with an old war buddy."

Bash nodded, maintaining a poker face even as his little soldier was ready to leap into battle in the presence of such a worthy adversary.

Carrot nodded happily and sat down on the empty chair next to him with a graceful motion.

"It's been a long time. How long, exactly?"

"Ever since the Rina Desert withdrawal campaign?"

"Oh, that's right! Ah, that takes me back..."

Carrot the Breathstealer.

Her personality was cold and calculating, brave and brutal.

She performed both hand-to-hand combat and magic at a high level. She was also said to have evenly matched Thunder Sonia in battle.

She was a veteran succubus who always fought on the front lines. She had also been an elite member of the succubus army. When even the weakest succubus soldier was a force to be reckoned with, being recognized as an elite put into perspective just how dangerous Carrot could be.

Her name was known far and wide, especially in the elf army, where she was both feared and despised as the one who'd captured the largest number of elf men.

"Hee-hee, it truly is an honor, Sir Bash."

Carrot lifted her glass to Bash's.

The glasses clinked loudly.

"The honor is mine."

But though Bash said that, he did his best to look at Carrot as little as possible.

Humans who didn't know much about the relationship between orcs and succubi might have wondered why someone like Bash was acting so demure in front of such a hypersexual woman.

However, you could hardly blame Bash.

Succubi saw men of other races as a food source. First, they captivated them with their sultry appearances, and then, once they'd seduced them into the ideal scenario, they *sucked* their sustenance from their prey. While other races considered sex an act of pleasure, propagation, or both, succubi quite literally could not live without it.

And most importantly, sex with a succubus would never produce a child.

When succubi wanted children, they kissed each other. While their mouths were instrumental in harvesting that which sustained them, a succubus's mouth was also their reproductive organ.

At any rate, if a woman could not produce children, she could not be the ideal wife to an orc.

But more than fathering children, Bash's most fervent desire was to lose his virginity.

As long as he could have sex, what did the finer details matter? ...One might think.

But matter they did.

A tale from the past should suffice for an explanation.

This is a tale from long ago... Long before Bash had even been born.

There once was an orc.

This orc had red skin, branding him a red orc. His physique had been splendid since birth, and he had a promising future ahead of him, having defeated an orc two years older than him the very first time he wielded a sword.

This orc came back from his first battle with a woman in tow.

She was a succubus. The two had hit it off on the battlefield, and after teaming up to annihilate their common enemy, they spent the night together and returned home a couple.

Thus, the orc married the succubus.

For orcs, intercourse that could not result in children was considered a tragic waste of seed. However, sex with a succubus was said to be the best one could ever hope to have.

Orcs preferred to display the naked bodies of their wives, and the act of their vigorous lovemaking, publicly, that other orcs may look on in awe and envy.

Marrying a succubus wasn't something that just anyone could do, so the red orc held his head high and enjoyed a life of pride. It seemed the other orcs were also very jealous of the man who could enjoy the love of a beautiful succubus to the fullest.

However, that happiness was destined to come to an end one fateful day.

As the hapless red orc was strutting through the village one day, he noticed a strange sensation.

Folks who'd been interacting normally with him until as recently as the day before were now approaching him with a surprised, scornful, somewhat unfamiliar attitude, as if he was a walking, suppurating boil.

The red orc was puzzled and questioned one of his friends. The friend, solemn-faced, brought the red orc a polished mirror.

When the orc looked into the mirror, he saw a familiar face.

But there was something unfamiliar on the orc's forehead.

No, not quite unfamiliar. He had seen it before. If anything, there were times when he himself had pointed at it and laughed, times when he had ridiculed the one who bore it.

The moment he realized it was attached to his body, he felt his blood run ice-cold.

It was a brand that every orc mage had.

The mark of...a wizard.

The crest of virginity branded the red orc's forehead.

It had been his thirtieth birthday that day.

From that day onward, the red orc and his succubus wife were never seen again.

In orc society, it is considered a terrible shame for warriors to become spellswords or wizards.

No matter the circumstance...

Therefore, the man probably left the village out of a sense of unbearable embarrassment and died of shame somewhere.

This one tale had been passed down in orc territory for generations. It was said that for some reason, no matter how many times a virgin had sex with a succubus, their chastity would not waver in the slightest.

Additionally, it was said that if an orc virgin's first time was with a succubus, then no matter how often they had sex with other women afterward, the crest of virginity would still manifest on their thirtieth birthday.

"..."

For these reasons, Bash never once made a move on Carrot.

If Bash had even hinted at the desire to sleep with her, she likely would have been more than happy to oblige.

He could finally experience the act of sex. And if he asked Carrot to be his wife, he could probably live a blissful life like the red orc from the tale.

But that would mean the end of Warrior Bash.

Furthermore, it would mean the birth of Magic Warrior Bash. Bash the Virgin Wizard.

For him, that was tantamount to the end of the world.

"It's cruel irony, isn't it? I'm the strongest succubus soldier, and you're an unbeatable Orc Hero. It's in our nature to upend our adversaries and savor the spoils of battle. Yet here we both are, desperately hunting for a mate."

"Indeed."

Carrot, for her part, did not approach Bash more than necessary.

She didn't wrap her arms around him, she didn't press her chest against him, she didn't put her mouth to his ear and whisper.

Any man was a viable food source for a succubus. However, succubus culture also frowned upon treating valued males like prey. Bash was much more than a meal to Carrot.

"Sometimes, I miss the war. We could capture as many men as we wanted and devour their essence as we pleased... Now we're like rats scavenging for whatever we can find..."

"..."

"I want to go back to that time... I think fondly of the days when we were able to live and die freely...even though there were periods when we struggled... Don't you miss it?"

"..."

Bash did not answer.

If, at this very moment, all treaties were scrapped and war began anew, Bash would lose his virginity in a heartbeat. He'd go straight to the human country, find Judith, capture her, and indulge himself without a second thought.

But that was a pipe dream.

Currently, if war were to break out, the orcs would be wiped out in the blink of an eye.

The Orc King Nemesis wanted the orc species to persist. Peace was a necessity.

War was the last thing Bash should have hoped for.

"Hee-hee, just kidding..."

"Ah."

"But if the opportunity ever does come around again, I do hope you'll allow me the honor of fighting by your side once more."

Her words resurrected past battles in Bash's mind.

The withdrawal from the Rina Desert.

In that battle, the succubus army was cornered. The Rina Desert was now part of beastkin territory, but it had once been part of the lizardfolk's desert territory.

The territory had been seized in an invasion, the aggressors being a mixed army of dwarves and humans.

The succubi, who fought alongside the lizardmen, fought with all their might to protect their allies.

However, most of the lizardmen, who preferred to live in marshy areas, actually disliked deserts.

Succubi were also poorly suited to fighting in the wide-open vistas of the desert.

Originally, a mixed army of ogres and harpies was assigned to the defense of the Rina Desert, but after the death of Geddigs, both ogres and harpies became too busy defending their own territories and withdrew from the desert.

And so those who remained were trapped there.

The orcs went to help the lizardmen and succubi, who were driven into a corner by the dwarves.

However, the battle line had already collapsed, and the combined army of sandy lizardmen and succubi was completely surrounded and nearing annihilation.

Thus, the withdrawal battle of the Rina Desert.

In that confrontation, Bash showed his usual mettle and saved the succubi and lizardmen.

The woman next to him now had been in command of the succubus army at the time.

Bash remembered it well, too.

After the dust of battle cleared, she had been there, standing by his side.

Few words were exchanged between them. Two or three at most. Bash didn't even remember them.

However, there weren't many who could say they remained standing next to the Orc Hero Bash at the end of a fierce battle.

Most couldn't keep up and dropped out, deserted, or were killed in action.

Being able to keep up with Bash was proof of a first-class warrior, with a great deal of hidden power.

This was why he had no trouble recognizing Carrot.

That...and he also remembered the heaving breasts that swayed every time she dealt a blow... But Bash decided to shake the memory of those breasts for now.

It would be a bad idea to dwell on the memory of her full appearance right this moment.

There would be time for that later, after he'd safely disposed of his virginity.

If the two of them could have the fortune of meeting again *after* he'd done the deed, he was positive they'd be able to enjoy a mutually beneficial relationship.

"Of course. It would be an honor to fight again alongside you as well."

"...Hee-hee, thank you."

Carrot smiled.

Most of her face was hidden, but he could tell that her smile was charming even beneath the mask.

If he hadn't known Carrot was a succubus, Bash would have proposed to her.

The succubus race constantly emitted pheromones that effortlessly attracted men.

But Bash knew about the pheromones, so he was able to hit the brakes on his biological response.

"I still remember your bravery. The dwarf warlord Goldoroff charged from the flank, everyone thought they were done for, and both succubi and lizardmen screamed in terror. While I was being attacked, only you calmly came to assist."

"You didn't run away, either."

"Hee-hee, I'm honored to receive the compliment... But in truth, I felt the same as the rest. I wanted to run away... I was terrified... But I had to put on a brave face for my people..."

For a while, Bash and Carrot simply sat and reminisced.

At first, Bash was nervous that she might ask him about his past exploits with women, but gradually, he found himself beginning to talk about his achievements and battles with an eloquence he'd never managed back at the bars and taverns of his hometown.

Carrot was very easy to talk to.

They drank without reservation, and the conversation flowed like water.

If this woman weren't a succubus… But no, even if she was a succubus, and if Bash himself were not a virgin, then he would have loved to take her right then and there.

He wouldn't have minded being food if this woman was the one doing the eating. She understood him. He would've loved to be with her forever.

There was no way for the virgin Bash to know that Carrot might have been playing him. Perhaps if he had studied the tactics of women of the night, he would have been wise to her tricks.

By the way, Zell was currently sleeping with their arch nemesis, Bowl of Almonds, on the counter table. After settling their differences following a quarrel and a drunken brawl, they were now lovers. Bowl of Peanuts? They were old news.

"There's so much left to talk about, but let's leave it here for tonight."

"Okay." ·

If Carrot was truly aiming to *have dinner* with Bash, surely she wouldn't have suggested they separate.

No, she would have slowly leaned over Bash's shoulder, pressed her ample chest against him, and told him with glistening eyes that she was drunk. Then Bash wouldn't have been able to resist. He would have been the one to suggest that he take Carrot home. And then his goose would have been cooked.

Or if Bash *weren't* a virgin, he would have whispered sweet nothings to entice Carrot himself. A succubus cannot conceive a child, true. But was not Bash a proud orc? Who was going to tell him he couldn't mate with the woman of his choosing?

"Hee-hee, let's see each other again. Soon, I hope."

But things didn't quite pan out that way.

Carrot remained a polite succubus until the end, and Bash remained a virgin.

"Let's."

Bash said his good-byes, his nose filled with the lingering scent of Carrot's pheromones. As to whether he was drunk on booze or the pleasant conversation he'd had with a ravishing remnant of his past…who can say?

5

The Masked Saint, Aurantiaca

The heart of Lycant. The royal palace, Lycaon.

The garden, building, and interior were all brand-new, beautifully decorated with gold, silver, and jewels for the third-born princess, who was getting married.

And that's not all.

A month had gone by since the third-born princess's marriage was announced with a huge fanfare, and preparations for the wedding were progressing steadily.

Innuella, the third-born beastkin princess, was to wed Captain Aconitum, an elf soldier.

It was a very auspicious event, even from a global perspective.

The marriage was not only considered very lucky but also politically significant, as it strengthened the ties between the two countries and, at the same time, was intended to keep other countries in check.

Accordingly, the elf and beastkin royal families were giving all they had to make sure the wedding was the most lavish event the world had seen following the long war.

Splashing about their wealth, they held festivals, spread word the world over, and packed the invite list with high-profile individuals.

But of course, not everyone was pleased.

One such party was the human aristocrats, who did not want the elves and beastkin to gain more power. The dwarf merchants were also displeased. They had been left out of the loop and missed a significant moneymaking opportunity. The last of the disgruntled groups were the elf factions who stood in opposition to Aconitum and his clan.

■   ■   ■

"...So in other words, if you use this trick, once it's speculated that poison is the cause, a suspect without an alibi will come forward! Yes, indeed!"

In a room within Lycaon Palace, there was uproar.

The big names from each country who were invited to the wedding had gathered together and were listening to a single woman speak.

Judging by her long blond hair and pointed ears, she must have been an elf.

But her face was hidden behind a mask, and her true identity could not be discerned.

Everyone there knew who she was, of course. But at the same time, they did not. There was a tacit understanding about it, you see.

"Bougainvillea."

"...!"

The masked woman cornered another woman.

She had short blond hair and long ears. One ear was adorned with a large earring. The masked woman clutched the other earring in her hand.

"Speak! Why did you try to do this? Aconitum is your childhood friend, isn't he?"

Bougainvillea.

The woman by that name looked down, trembling.

But before long, she raised her head defiantly and cried out.

"...What do you know?! You've been a virgin for hundreds of years!"

"Hey! Enough of that!"

"I've loved Aconitum for ages! I've made our meetings between fierce battles my heart's comfort! Once the battles were over, I dreamed I'd finally be able to be with him. How can he be marrying some furry animal, in such a beastly smelling palace?! I won't stand for it!"

"What does any of that have to do with my virginity?!"

"For dear Aconitum, I would accept any mission no matter the severity! If I was ordered to, I would kill old people and even children! But I planned to go straight after marriage! Because I love him so! But I was told that if a royal was to marry the former leader of an assassination squad, it would sully his reputation! And since I was captured and assaulted by orcs during the war, my body is no longer desirable! You couldn't possibly understand how I feel! You could never understand the cruel hand of fate I've been dealt!"

"But I do understand! I do... I mean, even I..."

"How could you possibly understand? You... You loveless virgin!"

"Um, do you remember how I was captured by an orc and later released unmolested because I... Because I apparently smell? How do you think that made *me* feel, hmm?"

"That orc *proposed* to you! And for a moment, you were completely swept up in the idea!"

"Uh...um... Ah well, I suppose that's true. Yeah. I guess I don't understand your feelings... I'm sorry..."

The masked woman broke into a cold sweat and apologized, clearing her throat.

"Anyway! You let that anti-Aconitum faction take advantage of you and use you as a patsy, hmm?"

The masked woman fiddled with the earring.

A drop of liquid spilled out from the tip.

A sinister purple liquid. It appeared to be a deadly poison.

"..."

"You know... Maybe they don't understand your feelings, either?"

Bougainvillea's expression became shrouded in mystery as she glared at the masked woman who'd been choosing her words so carefully.

Not that it mattered. They were well past the point of no return.

Aconitum was not present, but it had already been revealed that she was trying to assassinate a member of the beastkin nobility in order to force a cancellation of the wedding.

Her future was forfeit.

"Then I suppose I have no choice..."

Bougainvillea withdrew a dagger from her bosom.

A sinister, twisted dagger. A badge of honor, given to those who had made particularly outstanding achievements in the elf army's assassination squad.

Bougainvillea, the finest assassin in the assassination unit, unleashed her bloodlust.

"Wha—? Hey, stop! Don't do something rash!"

"I'll kill you all! Innuella and Aconitum, too! And yes, even you! I won't allow this...this farce of a marriage to proceed! I'll destroy everything!"

The entire area erupted into chaos.

Some drew swords, some channeled their magical power.

Bougainvillea was alone, even though she'd been the finest assassin in the assassination squad. Those in attendance were all brave soldiers who'd survived the war. Many of them were as strong as or more powerful than Bougainvillea. She had no chance of winning.

"Hey, Bougainvillea. It's true that I don't understand your feelings. But I've known you and Aconitum since you were little. I didn't realize you had feelings for Aconitum, but I know you're not a bad person! You've always been strong, and you always protected him from bullies..."

Bougainvillea's eyes glistened as she listened to the masked woman speak.

"It's sad that your love went unrequited. Those people who made you feel unclean after everything you sacrificed for the elves... I'll put a burning hex on them. Or if you want, I can personally praise your achievements in public. Yes, I should have done that from the start! I was so preoccupied with myself that I didn't even spare a thought for how you might have suffered. Please forgive me."

The voice of the masked woman brought Bougainvillea back to happier times.

A long time ago, when she'd quarreled with one of her peers and ended up crying, this masked woman had similarly come to offer her words of comfort.

For the elves who'd lost their parents in the war, this masked woman was a sort of mother figure, a teacher. Someone worth protecting at all costs.

"Let us find you a new man to love. Yes. For example, how about Cymbidium? He was also a member of the assassination squad, was he not? He's still single, isn't he? All right, he might not be all that impressive compared to you, but he's not a bad guy, either. Why not consider him as a romantic prospect? I'll even help you. Okay?"

The masked woman spoke soothingly and slowly approached.

She moved carefully, so as not to startle Bougainvillea. Her aim was to snatch away the dagger safely.

But her words were sincere. She was deeply concerned for Bougainvillea.

"...!"

Suddenly, Bougainvillea realized what she was doing.

She was pointing her blade at someone she should never point her blade at.

Pointing a blade at a national treasure, the mother of all elves.

"So come on. Can you give me that dagger?"

The masked woman gently touched Bougainvillea's cheek.

At this gentle touch, Bougainvillea felt all her strength leave her.

The dagger clattered to the floor.

"...Sorry ...I'm so sorry."

She sobbed, tears flowing from her eyes and snot from her nose.

And so a harrowing incident and an unrequited love both came to an end.

■　　■　　■

That evening, the masked woman was drinking fruit wine in one of the guest rooms at Lycaon Palace.

"..."

She thought back to that scene earlier in the day.

Today, one of the guests invited to the wedding had nearly been poisoned.

Although the attempt was thwarted, if the guest had died, the wedding might have been called off. Or perhaps there would have been a war between the beastkin and the elves.

"That was too close..."

The culprit was someone the masked woman knew well.

Bougainvillea.

She had known her since childhood. Well, actually, the masked woman knew the vast majority of the elves' names, faces, and backgrounds, but let's put that aside.

Bougainvillea was a hopeless girl, but thanks to the persuasion and pleas of the masked woman on her behalf, it seemed unlikely that she would be sentenced to death. Still, she could not avoid a suitably harsh punishment.

The masked woman thought back to the things Bougainvillea had said while she was being backed into a corner.

Honestly, they resonated with the masked woman.

Her chest still hurt.

"Why is Aconitum so popular...?"

She sipped her drink as she muttered to herself.

She wore a thick belly warmer over her pajamas, which had not even a shred of sex appeal, and was collapsed sloppily in her chair.

"Yeah?"

There had been a knock at the door.

The masked woman called out, still sloppily slumped.

"Who is it? It's open, you know!"

"It's me. I'm sorry I'm late."

It was a man's voice. She knew this man, too.

The masked woman leaped over to the door with a speed she'd only demonstrated once or twice on the battlefield and held on to the twisting doorknob for dear life.

"Oh? It doesn't seem like it's open?"

"I'm sorry, I just locked it. Yeah. Please wait there for a moment. I'll open it right away."

"All right."

From there, the masked woman acted quickly.

She yanked off her pajamas and belly warmer at super-high speed and threw them into her bag.

Then she changed into the sheer loungewear she'd prepared in case of guests. Freezing, she muttered, "No, no, too risqué," and grabbed a cardigan from her bag to throw on over it.

She checked herself out in the full-length mirror to make sure she looked sexy but understated. Nodding, she reclined in the chair she'd been sitting on earlier and picked up her glass of fruit wine.

"O-okay... You can come in now."

"Oh, did you unlock it?"

"It's open."

There was a hint of a wry smile in the voice that was coming from the other side of the door, but the masked woman didn't know why.

After all, it was the first time a man other than a blood relative had visited her at such a late hour, so you could hardly blame her for being nervous.

"Pardon my intrusion."

"Ah, hello... Huh?"

The masked woman was at a loss for words for a moment.

From the voice, she had a pretty good idea of who was on the other side of the door. And when the person walked in, her suspicions were confirmed.

He wore a mask meant to look like a woman's face.

"Hey, what's with the weird mask? Is that your idea of a joke?"

"What about you, Thunder Sonia? Wearing a mask, alone in your own room...?"

"Gah! Idiot! Shhh! Right now, I'm the Masked Saint, Aurantiaca. Thunder Sonia is not here!"

"Up to that old trick again, are you...?"

"Think about it! if people found out I was coming, wouldn't Aconitum get all flustered? Like changing the seating order, or upgrading me to a fancy suite... He must be busy enough preparing for his wedding! He doesn't have time to pander to me!"

"I see."

The masked man nodded, though the grin did not leave his face.

Thunder Sonia originally wore her mask during the war. It was the kind of mask that amplified her magical power.

So it was more natural for her to wear one around those she didn't know well.

If she wore the mask and went about normally, no one would suspect it was her in disguise.

With the mask on, people would go along with her wishes if she told them she didn't want special treatment because of her being Thunder Sonia.

"And what's the story behind *your* mask, hmm?"

"My reasoning is similar to yours. Right now, I am the emissary of love and peace, Errol... But all that aside, today was very impressive. You protected that girl from the shadows."

"Hmph, well, she's one of my own. It was up to me to clean up after her mess."

"It appears you've been doing this kind of service all over."

"The war may be over, but there are too many of my kinsmen who are disgruntled."

The masked woman...or rather, Thunder Sonia, heaved a sigh.

She'd set out from the Shiwanashi Forest, and since then, she'd been searching far and wide for a good man.

First, she tried the human country, then the land of the elves, but she had no luck in either place.

Apparently, the elves had been causing trouble in various places ever since the war ended.

In particular, there was fierce strife between Prince Aconitum, who was expected to be the next king, and Prince Erigeron, who was plotting to wrest the throne from Aconitum. And their quarrel was not only domestic but extended as far as them attempting to gain the most foreign allies.

Thunder Sonia intervened every time she caught wind of trouble, but as a result, rumors began to spread that she was traveling around incognito and judging the wrongdoings of her people.

In truth, she was just trying to find herself a man!

"So what's this all about, *Errol?* If you keep carrying on like this, and visiting maidens' bedrooms in disguise, rumors are going to start flying about, you know? You'll be chased by the Elf Intelligence Department, forcibly stripped of your mask, and held personally liable."

In her mind, those words were an invitation for him to take off the mask, answer to his real name, and take responsibility for...well...whatever was to transpire between them this night.

Or preferably every night, and not just this one.

But she was beating about the bush to such an extent that he could hardly be blamed for not picking up on her advances.

"...That's right. Certainly, I didn't think carefully enough about how my late-night visit to the virgin Saint Aurantiaca might be perceived. I'll be sure to leave as soon as I've conducted my business."

"Ah... I see. Yeah... You do that..."

Unable to withdraw her previous words, Thunder Sonia felt herself physically shrinking.

She had been expecting the man to advance on her and purr, *So it's okay, as long as I take responsibility...?* But no sensible man would risk a frivolous nighttime fling with Thunder Sonia, the elven figurehead. Even the most shameless man wouldn't be stupid enough to risk laying a hand on her.

"There is a little something I would like to whisper in your ear."

"What?"

"They have begun to move, as expected."

Thunder Sonia frowned.

"Is that so?"

"They may have already invaded this country, too."

"What about the wedding? Should we cancel it?"

"Until we know what their aim is, there is little we can do... But it seems the Queen intends to move forward with everything."

"That doesn't surprise me in the slightest... The Queen can be so stubborn... So what am I supposed to do?"

"For the time being, we are only providing information and forewarning those who are likely to be able to act when the time comes."

"...I see. Thanks for the information. So proceed with caution...is that all?"

"That is all."

"Is that really all?"

"That is really all."

"I see..."

Thunder Sonia's brain was working fast.

This man was Errol, the emissary of love and peace.

Thunder Sonia was aware that he was single.

She knew the face behind the mask was handsome. She knew his pedigree, his glorious battlefield exploits, and so on.

He wasn't a bad prospect at all.

"Well, it's a wedding we all want to see happen. Let's make sure it goes off without a hitch! I'll do what I can on my end!"

"Happy to hear it."

"D-don't you get excited by the thought of weddings or, um, celebrations? Hmm? I mean, if you were to get married, there would be much excitement all across the world, wouldn't there? If you don't have a partner in mind, though, that is to say, I..."

"There is a woman who's been on my mind."

Thunder Sonia fell silent at this.

She hesitated to ask who the woman was.

Such knowledge might deal her a fatal blow.

"I—I see... Well then, it's fine as long as you have a partner. Yeah."

"Indeed. Excuse me, then."

"Oh, yeah. I understand. I'm sorry I kept you so long..."

"Do be careful, Thunder—I mean...Aurantiaca."

"Of course. I am Thunder Sonia, the grand elf mage! I will be careful. Oh yes, very careful."

Errol bowed and headed for the doorway.

Thunder Sonia bit her lip as she watched him go. Maybe she could still call him back?

Then Errol stopped.

"Ah, I almost forgot."

"Wh-what is it?!"

"The Orc Hero has come to town."

"Bash?"

"He must have come to celebrate the princess's wedding."

"I see..."

Thunder Sonia was shaken to hear the Orc Hero's name.

But come to think of it, it wasn't so strange that Bash was there.

Considering the friendship between orcs and beastkin...this wedding was the perfect opportunity.

"Perfect formal attire, modest demeanor... And it seems like he was holding back on the booze so as not to lose his decorum. It was as if he was very aware of how he would come across to the beastkin royals. Not the kind of thing most orcs have the capacity for."

"Right? When he came to propose to me, he was dressed in elven attire. I refused, of course! I mean, naturally!"

Originally, orcs would never bow to the families of those they'd killed on the battlefield.

It was far more likely for an orc to say something like, *I'll kill you, too, until there isn't a single member of your bloodline left...!*

But Bash was prepared to bow his head for the sake of his clan's pride and honor.

Of course, Bash's actions were a little different than a normal apology.

Wearing the formal attire of another tribe, appearing at formal occasions, and proudly delivering a congratulatory address...

It was a demonstration... A demonstration that said: *We orcs respect other races and wish you no harm.*

"However, the beastkin royal family doesn't seem to be as intelligent as the Orc Hero. While I was out of the room, it seems he was cruelly treated and kicked out. Ah, I only wish I'd been there."

"What...? Are the beastkin royals stupid? I understand how they feel, yes, but that's no way to behave. They hold on to grudges for far too long. The war is over, and everyone's trying to get along, but they cling to their hatred of orcs alone? What are they, children?!"

"You're right... But if, for example, you were killed by the Nightmare of the Shiwanashi Forest, I think the elves would have reacted much the same."

"Ah... Well, we've got plenty of our own naughty, wayward children."

Errol chuckled.

Even coming from Thunder Sonia, it was funny to hear elves who had lived hundreds of years being referred to as children.

"I hope the Orc Hero does not hold a grudge of his own and that he will not consider taking revenge."

"No... I don't think he would do such a thing. Even after being turned down by me, he just dusted himself off and moved on to the next town... I doubt another orc would react with as much civility."

"I hope that's the case... But I worry about *them* and the way in which they're heading... Thunder Sonia, you must be careful, too."

"Of course. You really think I'd ever let my guard down, hmm?"

"Heh, I suppose I shouldn't have to worry about you of all people. Well then, excuse me."

Errol bowed once more and took his leave.

Thunder Sonia, alone in the room, drained her glass of fruit wine and then flung herself over the table.

She'd be lying if she said she wasn't worried about *them* as well, to say nothing of her mounting curiosity after learning Bash was in attendance as well.

But what had shocked her most was…something else.

"Gah…"

Thunder Sonia heaved a huge sigh, then, still sprawled over the table, muttered in an almost inaudible voice.

"*Of course* a man like that has a woman in his life…"

Thunder Sonia sighed again. Ever since she'd set out on her journey, it had been nothing but dead end after dead end…

6

Ladies Love a Man Who Can Wait

"It's morning already?"

When Bash woke up at the inn, he stretched his taut muscles and then got dressed.

He splashed hot water over himself, spritzed on some cologne, and donned the formal attire of the beastkin.

After some breakfast on the inn's ground floor, he returned to his room. He sat down on the bed, folded his arms, and closed his eyes.

He felt great.

Yes, the best battle strategy was to follow the orders of a skilled tactician.

That always worked for him when the Demon Lord Geddigs was alive. Bash was able to win all the battles just by following the orders that came from the top.

Without that Demon Lord's guidance, Bash wouldn't be as strong as he was now. It was entirely possible that he wouldn't even have lived to see this day.

"Think opportunity will come a-knocking today, Boss?"

Zell was munching on a pile of almonds for breakfast and filling a small bottle with fairy dust.

He had a lot of almonds left over. No doubt today's fairy dust would be almond flavored.

Bash made no move.

He didn't go out, and he didn't train. He just sat still.

No girl hunting, no going to bars.

"Just waiting around is surprisingly easy."

He was waiting.

For what, you ask?

Opportunity.

In other words, for the natural passage of time.

Bash waited. The other day, he'd met that superb beastkin girl, Silviana. He had no doubt she would come for him, as she said she would.

After all, that's what the magazine said.

IF A GIRL WANTS TO SEE YOU AGAIN, DON'T RUSH IT! DON'T GET ALL PUSHY! LADIES LOVE A MAN WHO CAN WAIT!

The secret to beastkin dating was all in the waiting period.

That's what the magazine said. So Bash decided to wait. Bash, who blazed a trail across every battlefield in the world, was renowned for his overwhelming direct attacks. But he was actually also very good at ambushes.

If necessary, he could wait in a thicket for ten to twenty days.

Even if the enemy never came, he wouldn't feel bitter at all.

And today, he was waiting for his future bride.

There was no pain in waiting. On the contrary, it only made the flames of passion burn brighter within him.

"…"

So Bash was waiting.

From the day of that unpleasant scene in that palace until now.

From sunrise, he did not stir, even when the sun was directly above him in the sky. He did not stir, even when the sun began to move across the heavens. He ate again when the sun was setting, but after that, he resumed his vigil. After the town had fallen asleep, Zell and he would take turns standing guard and waiting.

Several days had gone by in this manner.

Bash was going to bathe for a second time today, eat dinner, and then wait in bed at the inn.

After waiting this long, it would probably occur to most people that the person they were waiting for was not coming. But Bash had been successful in ambushing his prey even after waiting an obscenely long time.

Such an ambush had even allowed him to defeat Kuderlandt, the Trampling King.

So Bash continued to wait.

No doubt, he would wait forever. Forever and ever, day after day, into eternity...

And before you knew it, the third-born princess's wedding would be over. The town's enthusiasm for all things weddings would cool. And before Bash even knew what had happened, the mark of the virgin would appear on his forehead for all to see.

He would realize that the woman had lied. That she was not coming after all...

But it didn't play out like that.

"So she's come."

That afternoon, a certain individual visited the inn.

Bash, with his senses on high alert, as they always were during battlefield ambushes, realized it immediately. Unfamiliar footsteps had just entered the inn.

After exchanging a few words with the proprietor of the inn, the owner of the footsteps came straight to Bash's room.

Judging from the length of the person's stride, it was a woman. The footsteps were quiet but not intentionally muffled. Whoever it was, they walked like a noble.

No doubt about it. It was her.

"Boss! You've made it this far. You can't afford to screw it up now!"

"I know. I will make her mine."

Princesses were the most desired conquests for orcs.

Aside from female knights, princesses never failed to come up in orc conversations about mating prospects.

However, princesses were few and far between. Unlike knights, they hardly ever appeared on the battlefield. And on the rare occasion that they did, they were never there long, as royals were quick to retreat when outmatched. Pursuing them was also risky, as they would be defended by a heavily armed rearguard.

Even if an orc managed to get past the guards, many princesses would sooner take their own lives as a last resort rather than be defiled by an orc.

Princesses were often seen but rarely conquered.

As such, they were like rare and exotic fruit.

As far as Bash knew, there were only a handful of orcs who had even been able to marry a princess.

And most of these accounts were little more than fairy tales. Only one living orc had been known to conquer a princess: the Orc King, Nemesis. But the princess in question was no longer alive.

Silviana, the fifth-born beastkin princess, would do nicely as the wife of the Orc Hero Bash.

An opportunity like this one might never come around again.

Thinking about it made Bash's spirits soar higher than ever.

"...Hmm."

Then there came a knock at the door to Bash's room.

"Come in, it's open!"

At Zell's call, the door opened.

There stood a shadow in a modest yet clearly expensive silk robe, with a hood covering their face.

The face peeking out from behind the hood was the same beautiful face Bash had seen only once, the other day.

It was the fifth-born princess, Silviana.

The one he had waited for had come at last. The ambush had been a success.

"Hee-hee-hee."

She looked at Bash and smiled softly.

"My sudden visit seems to have caught you by surprise."

"Not at all."

"Huh?"

Silviana stiffened at Bash's words.

Indeed, on closer inspection, Bash's clothes were formal attire. The best clothes of the beastkin tribe, as if he was on his way to a ceremony. It was almost as if he had dressed up just to greet her.

"Hee-hee, you couldn't wait?"

"I've been waiting all this time."

"..."

In response to those majestic words, Silviana frowned just a little.

She wasn't quite following. However, her expression soon melted, and she sat down next to Bash on the bed.

Then she leaned on Bash's shoulder.

Bash's upper arm was sandwiched between two plump breasts.

"Oh, Lord Bash! My darling! How I love you!"

"I feel the same."

Silviana let go, lay down on the bed, and closed her eyes.

As if she was waiting for something. *I'm ready! Take me now!* ...was what her body language seemed to suggest.

"Then let us go."

Bash, however, stood up.

"Go? Where to?"

"Is it not obvious?"

Bash grinned at the confused Silviana.

His tusks sparkled.

"We are going on a date."

This was the winning method. It said so in the magazine, and the magazine hadn't been wrong yet.

■   ■   ■

SO SHE'S COMING ON TO YOU? DON'T MAKE THE SAME MISTAKE MOST MEN MAKE! FORGE A RELATIONSHIP FIRST!

THE ERA OF WOMEN LEADING THE WAY IS OVER! NOW THE MAN MUST TAKE THE LEAD WITH AN ENJOYABLE DATE!

According to the magazine, a beastkin love affair seemed designed to test the man's endurance.

It was not wise to push for a sexual encounter or marriage straight out of the gate.

Even if it looked like a woman was coming on hot and heavy, this was likely a trap.

If you flung yourself at the object of your desire, you would be slapped and rebuffed, with the angry woman declaring: *That wasn't what I was implying at all!*

To get to the bedroom stage, you had to smoothly proceed through the other stages first.

No stage could be skipped. First came dating. And dating, itself, had stages. Furthermore, there had to be at least five dates, with a different venue for each, as well as a variety of "lines" that had to be said.

After all this hard work, on the sixth date, you could propose and be guaranteed success.

Your beastkin babe would then be head over heels in love with you.

Honestly, without the magazine, Bash would have already made a fatal mistake.

Earlier, when Silviana leaned herself against him, Bash would have assumed the proposal was made and would have tried to hook up with her then and there. And then she would have slapped him away in the blink of an eye.

But Bash had the magazine.

Bash had also witnessed the downfall of frontline warriors acting on impulse when it came to delicate maneuvers.

As long as the plan was devised by an intelligent war strategist, following it to the letter was the key to victory.

Bash had experienced it firsthand.

Yes, it had been that way at the battle of Kian Plain.

Around that time, Bash himself was starting to get a little excited, and he had been growing in strength.

As usual, Bash was running east and west in accordance with his orders, destroying the enemy wherever he went.

Then Bash was given another order.

His task was simple. He was to ignore the enemy he was currently engaging with, travel south, and attack another enemy.

But Bash was caught up in the bloodlust of battle. How could he just turn tail and abandon a fight? He remained where he was.

As a result, their allies, the demon unit, were annihilated by a pincer attack. Bash's company was left alone and helpless.

In the end, Bash and his comrades survived, but they were severely berated by the demon commander.

This was a humiliating defeat that taught Bash a valuable lesson.

Since then, Bash had always obeyed orders.

Although, as time passed, and Bash grew stronger and collected more accolades, there were fewer and fewer people with the authority to give orders to him...

Anyway, Bash had made sure the itinerary for his first date with Silviana was perfect.

It was exactly as written in the magazine...

"Um, what is this place?"

"We will eat together here. Should we have gone to a different restaurant?"

"Ha-ha, no, I don't mind eating here... It's just..."

Taking the bewildered Silviana's hand, Bash entered the restaurant.

The magazine had recommended it, but the clientele were commonfolk, and the inside was cluttered and crowded.

It wasn't the sort of restaurant a princess would dine at.

But Bash had no way of knowing that.

"It seems the so-called *meat pie* comes highly recommended."

"You don't know what meat pies are, Lord Bash?"

"No. We don't have them in orc country."

"Is that so?"

In terms of atmosphere, it might not have been the best.

But Silviana laughed, sat down next to Bash, and clung to his arm. Then she gently stroked Bash's thigh.

"You impossible man... You mean to suggest that I'm the after-dinner dessert?"

"..."

Silviana's overt flirting made Bash a bit nervous, but he stubbornly adhered to the teachings of the magazine and made up his mind that he would hold out until he had done everything by the book.

Even among orcs, Bash's patience was second to none.

And Bash had recruited Zell as a deterrent in case he lost control.

Zell was there, watching Bash, sparkling away brightly in the corner of the restaurant.

Go for it, Boss! The future is bright!...was what Zell was thinking.

And so the meal ended without a hitch.

Afterward, Bash escorted her to the weapons shops mentioned in the magazine.

Beastkin women preferred strong men after all.

But now that the war was over, it was hard for a man to get by on strength alone.

So Bash's plan was to point out the strengths and weaknesses of each weapon at the shop, so she would know he wasn't simple like other men.

As Bash toured the weapon shops, he talked about the different features of the weapons they had on display.

But all of his intel had come from the magazine. Bash's personal knowledge was restricted to the occasional recollection of *Ah, I used this weapon on the battlefield once.*

To be honest, he couldn't deny that his weapons knowledge was limited. Bash didn't choose his own weapons, so he didn't really know which ones were good or bad.

But Silviana was smiling the entire time.

And when Bash talked about his memories of war, she nodded with pursed lips.

"This weapon is one that beastkin favor. It is called a katana. Very sharp."

"That's right. Beastkin practice the katana from childhood."

"The most impressive katana wielder I ever encountered was a man I met during the battle of the Remium Plateau."

"Aha, so there was another so brave as to stick in the memory of the great Bash? Well, who was it?"

"Leto the Brave."

Bash wasn't looking at Silviana's face when he spoke those words.

He narrowed his eyes at the blade of the katana, as if seeing a distant past reflected therein.

So he had no idea what kind of face Silviana had just made.

"He was an incredible warrior. He possessed a phantom sword with a swing arc that could not be read. His strength, martial skill, and speed made him a man worthy of the title of Hero. Had he not been gravely injured when I chanced upon him, I'm certain I would have been the one to lose my life."

"Such humility... But, Lord Bash, even if your enemy was in perfect health, you would never lose, right?"

"Even if I was able to secure victory in a battle against Leto at full health, it would have been far from easy."

"..."

Bash thought back to that fateful battle.

The battle that ended the war, in which Geddigs the Demon Lord died.

It was a fierce battle. Complete and utter chaos.

In the midst of that chaos, Bash heard reports that the Demon Lord was under attack, and so he ran quickly to the demon camp to protect the commander in chief.

However, he had been too late.

By the time Bash arrived, the Demon Lord Geddigs had already fallen.

And beside the corpses of the Demon Lord and his entourage stood a group of three—two men and a woman—who were getting ready to flee the enemy camp with their victory secured.

The Human Prince Nazar.

The Elf Archmage Thunder Sonia.

And the Beastkin Hero Leto.

Thunder Sonia had already drained her reserves of magical energy and passed out. Nazar was carrying her on his back.

The only way for them to break through the enemy lines was to defeat Bash.

Bash had no idea that the three were heroes of their respective nations.

He didn't even know their names.

However, he tried to kill all three of them.

No one ordered him to do this. Instincts told him it was the correct course of action.

However, two of the three escaped Bash's reach. Nazar was able to carry Thunder Sonia on his back and flee.

But why were they allowed to get away?

Because Leto the Brave stepped before Bash.

Although his body had been riddled with bleeding wounds, he roared and challenged Bash to single combat with all his remaining strength.

Of course, there was no way he could beat Bash in such a state, and so Leto perished that day.

"He fought honorably to the death so that his comrades could escape. Even though his strength was spent...even though he fell many times, he rose again and again until he could no longer. He fought to the bitter end, without ever once giving up. He was a true warrior. It was an honor to face him in battle and an even greater honor to claim victory."

"Then...why did you leave his body behind?"

"That much is obvious."

Bash spoke as if her question was rhetorical.

"As their final order, the Demon Lord's aides said, 'We cannot allow our enemies to see the Demon Lord's corpse.'"

Bash carried out the final request of his allies.

Bash was an orc, but he was also a warrior who had just survived a long battle.

Therefore, he understood that if the Demon Lord's corpse was found, the morale of his allies would drop.

He prioritized the victory of the entire army over his own honor.

Therefore, even though he knew it was disrespectful to the warrior who had fought to the death, he used the last bit of his strength to carry the Demon Lord's corpse away and left Leto's body where it lay.

He brought the Demon Lord Geddigs's body all the way back to the demon general.

In the end, the death of the Demon Lord Geddigs was reported by the Human Prince Nazar, and by the time Bash tried to return to the front line, the battle had already been settled, and retreat was underway.

He had no regrets.

He did what he had to do when Geddigs fell.

Even if Bash had held Leto's head aloft and roared over his victory, the end result of the war would have been the same.

"...So...that's what happened."

Silviana's voice was fainter than it had been before.

When Bash finally turned to face her, she still had a soft smile on her face.

While they enjoyed their window shopping, dusk fell.

People were starting to return to their homes or inns.

Among them, some who entered the inn huddled up close to a partner. Perhaps they were lovers.

Nighttime. Public time was over. Now it was time to get personal. In other words, for getting physical.

Perhaps Silviana sensed it, too. She leaned on Bash's shoulder and smiled shyly.

Bash noticed this and spoke to her.

"Did you have fun today?"

"Yes, Lord Bash. It was like a dream."

"In that case..."

Bash's eyeline went to the inn where he was staying.

Silviana's eyes went there, too.

As if she knew just where they were going next and just what they were going to do there, *together*. It was only natural that they—

"Well, let's call it here for today," said Bash.

"Um... What?"

Silviana's smile was frozen on her face.

"I'll take you to a much better place for our second date. Until then."

Bash walked away with a spring in his step and a twinkle in his eye.

In the twilight, tinged with long shadows, he strode away happily, without a hint of regret.

And soon, he was gone. Orc Heroes are also quick to withdraw.

"..."

Silviana was left there alone by the roadside.

"...Huh?"

Her mutter of surprise faded away into the twilight.

■　　■　　■

"Boss..."

When Bash returned to the inn, he was met with a solemn-faced Zell.

Zell, arms crossed and fists clenched, trembled for a moment, then eventually lifted their head and glomped onto Bash's face.

"You were *perfect*, Boss!"

"I agree."

Bash grinned.

His very first date.

Bash had felt the good vibes. Silviana was in a good mood the whole time, and by

the end of it, she was putty in Bash's hands. Bash didn't know much about romancing other races, to be sure, but he knew he'd made a good impression.

"If you ask me, Boss, that princess has already fallen head over heels for you! I bet if you wanted to, you could have brought her back to this inn this very night! She was giving you all the signs!"

"Maybe. But I can't let my guard down. The magazine said that some men trip right at the finish line."

"That's right! So far, sticking to the magazine has worked wonders! So let's just keep doing things by the book!"

Completely taken with Silviana, Bash's soldier was figuratively and *literally* ready to explode.

However, his strong spirit, which had allowed him to survive several battlefields, helped him suppress his urges.

This was all for the sake of his soon-to-be-lost virginity. This was all to get a wife and proudly return to his hometown as an Orc Hero. This was his final test.

If a Hero couldn't see the mission through to the end, who could?

"Boss, I'm gonna help you, too! I'm off to scope out places for the next date!"

"Thanks!"

"Anytime, anytime!"

Zell zoomed out the window.

No doubt the fairy would check every inch of every venue suggested in the magazine and bring a detailed report back to Bash.

From confirming the best route there to the specifics of the floor plans of the restaurant in mind, then finally negotiating with the head chef. All to make sure Bash's arrival was met smoothly.

Date two could not be allowed to end poorly.

...Sure, it sounded like a lot of work, but victory required effort.

As Bash looked up at the night sky, he thought back on his travels up to this point, his jaw slackening as he reminisced.

The following day, Bash's waiting period began again...

...is what one might have thought. But in truth, Bash didn't have to wait that long.

Silviana came the following day. And then again the day after that.

Bash met her with a cool smile and proceeded with the subsequent date plan, with Silviana practically melting for him each time.

Bash's ability to stay rational was pushed to its limits many times, but he never broke.

Because things were going exactly as planned.

If Silviana had abandoned Bash at any point, or if Bash had panicked, it might not all have gone this swimmingly.

Silviana was, indeed, extremely tempting.

She was handsy with Bash, murmuring sweet nothings and dropping countless innuendos about mating and pregnancy.

By all appearances, she was in love with Bash. By all appearances, she wanted to marry him and have his babies.

Everything was going just as it was written in the magazine.

Could a human strategist really predict the future to this extent?

There was no way this was a battle Bash would win so smoothly.

It was all going just a little bit too well.

■　　■　　■

They often say that when someone is experiencing success, someone else out there is experiencing difficulties.

"…"

It was late at night.

In one corner of Lycaon Palace, a woman was beating her fist against the wall.

Chewing away at on the nail of her left thumb, she was banging her right hand against the wall over and over.

"…"

Just bashing it against the wall, like some kind of mindless beast.

Her face was completely expressionless.

But if anyone was present to meet her eye, they would have caught a glimpse of pure hatred and anger burning there like hellfire.

7

Secret Maneuvers

Princess Silviana Rivergold, the fifth princess in line, was the tenth-born child of the royal beastkin Rivergold family.

Beastkin have many young, and royalty is no exception.

Her mother, Leona Rivergold, had given birth twice. The first time, she gave birth to five children, and the second time, six children.

Silviana was the fifth child of her mother's second pregnancy. The fifth of the second set of children.

She had been born on the battlefield.

Two years had passed since all the children of her mother's first birth died. Although the second set were long-awaited babies, their coming was not so fortuitous. At that time, the Demon Lord Geddigs was at his peak strength, and the beastkin race was on the verge of complete annihilation.

There were only a handful of royal retainers, and all showed pessimism about the dark future of the newly born princesses.

In the midst of all this, there was only one person who congratulated the Queen and honestly meant it.

Leto Rivergold.

Queen Leona's younger brother was the only one celebrating the birth of his nieces, the six princesses.

By the time the six princesses were born, their father was already gone, killed in the fighting.

Taiga Rivergold, the prince consort, had died in a battle that took place long before the six princesses were born.

The princesses' childhoods weren't exactly happy.

Battles and skirmishes. Yelling and screaming. They never knew a single day of peace.

Leto was something of an older brother figure to them.

Leto always protected them, and when they began to understand things more, he started to teach them combat techniques.

He might even have been a father figure, of sorts, to these fatherless girls.

They all admired, respected, and adored Leto.

And his recapture of the holy land only increased these feelings toward him.

The greatest and last counterattack of the beastkin tribe, an event that would be spoken of in legend for future generations, the very incident that turned Leto into Leto the Brave.

One of the few victorious battles they won against the Coalition of Seven under Geddigs's rule.

In that battle, Leto became a Hero.

For the six princesses, there was no finer hero in all the world.

At that time, everyone dreamed that one of the six princesses, who were all still young, would become Leto's wife in the future.

Such a dream would be shattered one fateful day.

The decisive battle of the Remium Plateau.

The brave Leto had voluntarily joined the death squad pursuing the life of the Demon Lord Geddigs, and he had died for it.

The six princesses survived the long war.

They were heartbroken, but many an honorable man had died in battle, and so they were able to take solace in that truth.

For those who worship the god of the hunt, there is no shame in defeat.

It was an honor for beastkin to be able to fight bravely and even to become a source of food for any who would defeat them.

...Yes, to become food.

But the Hero Leto was left to rot.

In all beastkin history, no one should have been more exalted than the humble fallen soldier.

This act of disrespect was impermissible.

Each of the six princesses polished her special skills and prepared for revenge.

They swore to themselves that when they entered the battlefield, they would kill the perpetrator, the orc warrior Bash.

But that opportunity never came, and the war ended.

Most of the princesses let go of their anger after the war.

In her position as the next in line to be queen, the first princess, Reese, thought war should be avoided and that they shouldn't hold a grudge against the orcs.

The third princess, Innuella, also started to look to the future after marrying the man she had admired since childhood.

They no longer had hatred in their hearts.

The other princesses held on to their hatred, but they had other important roles to play.

The second princess, Lavina, as the future queen's right hand, thought that, theoretically, they should not go to war with the orcs.

The fourth princess, Quina, as a future judiciary, thought that even if orcs appeared in their country, they should be treated fairly.

The sixth princess, Fululu, as someone who had inherited the skills of the Hero Leto, thought she should focus on passing down those skills to future generations.

All three were discriminatory toward orcs and privately thought that if an enemy orc should appear in front of them, they would kill it without a second thought. But should someone intervene at the last minute to stop them, they were rational enough to pause and listen to reason.

They were the beastkin princesses, and they were proud of their responsibility, guiding the next generation of beastkin.

But there was one other.

Only the fifth princess, Silviana, was different.

Silviana was the most beloved princess of the Hero Leto.

Because she was the most emotional and the biggest crybaby of the bunch, she often cried on the Hero Leto's lap.

She cried for various reasons. Bullied by sisters, bitten by dogs, stung by bees...

She was the most reckless of the six princesses and was the kind of person who didn't think much about the future.

When she came up with an idea, she put it into action, and it often ended in failure and with her in tears.

Mostly, it was her own fault, but Leto comforted her by stroking her hair every time she cried.

As she grew up, she studied hard and aimed to become a tactician.

It became her dream to lead the Hero Leto to victory with her strategy.

In aiming to become a tactician, she learned this lesson from Leto:

"A gentlehearted girl is not suited to be a battle strategist. Do you know why? Yes, that's right. It's because you can't afford to sympathize with your enemies *or* your allies. Tacticians sometimes drive their own allies to death and sometimes slaughter unsuspecting enemies. You have to be ruthless and stick hard to your purpose. And you have to understand well in advance what kind of result your strategy will produce. It may be difficult for you, but do you still think you can do it?"

Silviana nodded emphatically.

And more than Leto thought, she took those words seriously, stifled her own emotions, and began training to steel herself on the inside.

Now, before she took action on a certain idea, she would think hard about what the outcomes were likely to be.

As a result, she stopped crying all the time and became more cautious.

After continuing this training for a long time, she became the most coldhearted, the most cunning, and the most ruthless of the six princesses.

She endured Leto's death in this way. There were many days of crying and despair.

However, that was the last incident that ever affected her.

That day, she cast off the last of her emotions.

She put on a smiling mask and only spoke from a position of absolute logic.

The other princesses took pity on Silviana, who had been much changed, and worried about her.

But they relied on her, too.

Able to speak rationally without being overwhelmed by emotions, she was a great boon to the other princesses, who were easily overwhelmed by their own feelings.

...But that's neither here nor there.

The fifth-born princess, Silviana, was the most beloved princess of the Hero Leto.

And she was the one who adored Leto the most. Originally, she was the most emotional of all the princesses.

She was the one princess who took Leto's death and his besmirched pride more seriously than anyone else.

...And she was the most reckless.

But contrary to popular belief, she had not cast aside *all* her emotions. She had not hardened her deeply sentimental heart.

It was all just hidden deep down inside.

That's why, when an orc appeared in the royal palace, and she learned that it was the very same "Orc Hero" Bash who had killed Leto, she immediately devised a plan.

And this time, she would not bother to think about what might come next.

■

"..."

Silviana returned to the royal palace alone that day.

Wrapped in a modest yet well-made robe, head held high, she quietly stole through the darkness.

The guards of the royal palace recognized her on sight, but they dared not reproach her.

The groundwork had already been laid.

She returned to her room.

Normally, her maid would be running in to change her clothes for her, but there was no sign of anyone.

"..."

The moonlight illuminated the dark room.

Silviana slipped off her silk robe, showing soft, immaculate limbs.

If Bash were there, no doubt he would explode at this sight. Heroes were fragile things, too.

Then Silviana turned her face to the side.

She looked into a full-length mirror. In celebration of the end of the war, the Alliance of Four came together to create these special items, which were presented to the royal families of each country. This mirror had been adorned with several enchanted crests and would not lose its luster for a hundred years. Even if it were to be shattered with a club, it would repair itself in the blink of an eye.

She slammed her fist into this mirror.

Crick! An unpleasant sound resonated, and the mirror cracked.

The crack repaired itself instantly, as if time had been rewound, but Silviana slammed her fist into it over and over again.

Bloody smears marred the mirror's surface, but she kept on punching it.

Even when the cracking sound grew muffled, changed to a wet squishing sound, she continued.

Then, all at once, her madness tapered off.

Silviana's hand paused, her face blank, and she carefully wiped off the mirror with a cloth placed next to it.

Then she silently threw the cloth into the wastebasket, mumbled the incantation of a recovery spell in a low voice, and healed her wounded fist.

"..."

Silviana took out her night clothes from the closet, put them on, moved over to the window in the moonlight, and opened it.

She looked out at the inn Bash had returned to.

Her blank expression cracked like ice.

Her eyes reflected hatred, malice. She bared her teeth and let out a small growl.

"Proud to have fought him and won, are you?"

Her growl turned into an angry murmur.

Her murmuring was not only angry but somewhat confused, too.

She had believed things to be one way, only to find out they were another.

But no one heard her. Her voice melted into the nothingness of the dark night...

"..."

Silviana looked outside for a while longer, but eventually, she let out a small sigh and turned back to her room.

She wore a smile on her face.

Who was that smile for? What was that smile about? It was impossible to tell.

But the next moment, the smile froze upon her face.

* * *

"Hello there. Good evening."

Somehow, there was a woman in the room with her.

Sitting comfortably in a chair in the room, she was looking at Silviana with red eyes that shone brightly.

When did she get there? It was as if she'd appeared out of thin air.

Mere moments before, when she'd moved from the closet to the window, that chair had been empty.

The lights were off, so she couldn't see whoever it was. But Silviana instantly realized the person did not belong there.

"I don't remember inviting any guests."

Silviana brought her hand to her mouth.

Placing her index finger on her lips, she sucked in air.

This was known as the Call…a means of communication among beastkin.

The sound was audible only to certain beastkin ears. And ever since ancient times, it had proven useful as an emergency means of communication for the beastkin.

All beastkin were trained from childhood to be able to make the sound, even if they could not hear it themselves.

However, before Silviana could finish performing the Call, the intruder opened her mouth.

"Are you interested in a method to undermine the reputation of the Orc Hero?"

"…"

Silviana froze.

"You seem to be having a lot of trouble trying to get Bash entangled in your web…"

"…"

"That's right. Most orcs are nothing but brainless rogues, but those they call 'Heroes' don't give in to half-baked temptations or sweet talk. Even if the two of you were alone, he would never attack a princess out of carnal desire."

"What are you talking about?"

Before she knew it, Silviana was smiling again.

The smile that made everyone feel at ease. A poker face disguised as a smile.

"You don't need to say it. I know. You want to take revenge on Bash for killing the Hero Leto, right?"

"..."

"Your plan is to seduce him, lure him into the ideal scenario, claim he assaulted you, and try to ignite a new war against the orcs. Am I correct?"

"..."

She spoke in a flirtatious tone. It sounded almost as though she was joking.

However, what she was saying was true.

Those were, in fact, Silviana's true intentions.

Approach Bash, lure him into bed, make it seem like it was nonconsensual.

If she let him attack her, she could later cry, *I never had those kinds of intentions. I only approached him in the name of orc and beastkin friendship.* No matter what happened, she could make it seem as though Bash was at fault. Or so she thought.

She knew it was a weak sort of plan, but it was all she had.

She hadn't been expecting Bash to come to the beastkin country. Such an opportunity might never come again.

She had to go for it.

Even if Bash wasn't formally punished, it would have been good enough for her if the relationship between the beastkin and the orcs had broken down, or if the elf and human elites who were present went home with a bad impression of the orcs.

To have that, she didn't even care what happened to her body.

Never had she expected that she would have trouble enticing her prey.

"So what?"

Even if her true intentions had been sniffed out, Silviana would not budge.

She had been trained to stick to her guns. Anyway, she hadn't actually done anything yet.

It would be easy enough to claim she was only ever interacting with him in the first place for the sake of friendship between beastkin and orcs.

"You've admired Lord Leto for a long time. It was Lord Leto who taught you the basics of warfare. When you were captured and kept as a prisoner of war, likely to be killed, it was Lord Leto who saved you. It's only natural that you adore him. And he was the hero of all beastkin kind."

A smile escaped Silviana.

Then she composed herself again, her face hard as iron. Now she wore the ruthless expression the other princesses so feared.

"Even after the war ended, didn't you insist that the orcs should be destroyed?"

"...Sometimes, people change their way of thinking."

"Grudges don't disappear so easily. Trust me, I know. Bash. That rotten orc... He can't be allowed to get away with all he's done. Even though he left Lord Leto lying on the battlefield like trash, he lives a comfortable life. He even comes as a guest to Innuella's wedding. What a bothersome insect!"

As if enticed by those words, Silviana's expressionless mask melted away.

What appeared from under the mask was an expression of hatred and anger.

Yes. That's it. This woman was right.

He couldn't be allowed to get away with it.

The Orc Hero Bash needed to pay.

He was a devil. He deserved no mercy.

"...So what's the plan?"

"Hee-hee... Princess Silviana, one of the six beastkin princesses. Someone of your intellect should be able to figure it out, but... Would you like to hear my idea?"

"If you waste my time with nonsense, I'll kill you, too."

"Ooh, how scary."

Silviana moved toward the two red lights that had appeared out of nowhere in the room.

Her steps were filled with hate and rage.

"As for the method, it's very simple."

"War strategies should always be simple."

"Bash will be summoned to the wedding. You will try to seduce him, and I will charm him. Then Bash will be our puppet. As planned, you can have him try to force himself on you, or you can kill him with your own hands..."

"Charm him...? Do you mean to suggest you possess the magical skill of the succubi...?"

"Yes, as you can see…"

The moonlight illuminated the room.

The figure of the woman, who had only been vaguely visible until now, came into clear view.

She wore a leather top and skirt that clung to her body, just barely covering her private parts. She had wavy purple hair, shining red eyes, and a long tail.

"…I *am* a succubus."

The so-called charm of the succubi.

It was a form of magic that wreaked tremendous havoc during the war.

Once charmed, a victim was completely paralyzed from attacking the caster. On the contrary, they would then attack their allies.

The one drawback was that the ability was completely ineffective against women. However, if used on a man, unless they had a very high resistance to magic or were protected by some kind of magical talisman, they would become enthralled by the succubus.

These days, the elves, who fought a long campaign against the succubi, had fewer males than females in their population. It was believed they had the succubi to thank for that…

The charm was one of the forms of magic that was forbidden to use after the war.

Still, if you were to use it… Why, even an Orc Hero would not be able to resist.

"…What is it that you want?"

"I want you to let me touch the Sacred Tree."

"Touch the Sacred Tree? Is that all?"

"It's precious to us, too, you know? You beastkin aren't the only ones who believe in the god of the hunt."

Hearing this talk of faith, Silviana was convinced.

Every race worshipped their own deity, but during the long war, some crossed over into different sects. There were elves who believed in the spirits of iron and fire, and there were lizardmen who worshipped the sun god.

So some succubi believed in the god of the hunt, did they? Well, that wasn't the strangest thing she'd ever heard.

If this succubus had long lost access to an object of worship, as the beastkin once had, it would make sense that she would seek it and be willing to help bring Bash down to get what she desired.

"Come on, I'm begging you. When I went to ask for permission, I was flatly refused."

One could not approach the Sacred Tree without permission.

The guardians of the Sacred Tree, the ones who granted permission, would never let such an odd succubus get close.

No doubt a female guardian had been tasked with dealing with the succubus. But even among the beastkin women, there was still a strong prejudice against succubi.

Succubi were a vulgar race who cared only about sapping the vitality of men. It would not be surprising if the guardians wanted to keep such an individual away from the Sacred Tree.

Even ordinary believers were not allowed to approach it without some special reason.

Silviana herself was not without prejudice against succubi.

But her hatred for the orcs won out.

"Okay. I'm on board with your plan."

"Hee-hee-hee. Negotiations completed."

Silviana nodded blankly at the succubus, who had a bewitching smile on her face.

"Well then, I shall return on the day of the wedding. You won't double-cross me, will you?"

"That's *my* line."

The succubus fluttered the wings on her back and floated toward the open window.

Watching her back as she went, Silviana suddenly realized something.

She hadn't asked something important.

"By the way, what's your name?"

"Carrot. My name is Carrot."

Carrot the Breathstealer.

The strongest of the succubi, known to all warriors.

Silviana wondered why such a famed warrior would have come to her, but actually, her intrusion here made a lot more sense now.

A strong warrior should have found it easy to slip through security and sneak into her room.

"Yes. Thank you very much, Carrot."

"Indeed, Princess Silviana."

Carrot flew out of the room with another bewitching smile.

Darkness returned to the room.

"...?"

In the darkness, Silviana felt something strange.

There was an odd feeling in her heart, as if she'd forgotten something.

However, at the same time, she also felt somewhat refreshed, as if a haze in her mind had been cleared.

So she shook off the strange feeling.

Right now, she had to focus. She couldn't risk missing this once-in-a-lifetime opportunity to avenge Leto.

"The entire orc race should be exterminated..."

The sound of her muttering faded away into the dark of night.

8

The Wedding Venue

On the fifth date or later, if a girl invites you to a place with a sultry atmosphere, you'll know your opportunity to get closer to her has come!

On that day, a letter arrived for Bash.

The envelope was well-tanned leather trimmed with gold thread, with the beastkin royal family's crest emblazoned on the front of it.

Inside was a thick piece of paper covered in gold leaf.

And on it was written:

Tomorrow, the wedding of the third-born princess, my older sister, Innuella, will be held.

I envy my sister, whose union is blessed by everyone.

I believe that you and I may someday... Well, I think you know. But all my other older sisters have a grudge against the orcs.

If you and I get married, you will not be welcomed into the family. Our union will not be blessed.

So at the very least, on this happy day, let us meet under the full moon.

The moon will surely bless us.

Meet me beneath the Sacred Tree when Innuella's speech begins.

I write this wishing for the prosperity of orcs and beastkin alike.

–Silviana

If Bash and Zell had been uninformed, they wouldn't have understood the meaning of this letter. At best, they would have thought Silviana had something important to discuss beneath the Sacred Tree.

…But they had the magazine.

Yes, the magazine also detailed the truth behind the unique subtext used by the beastkin.

"Boss…"

"I know."

"Finally, the day has come."

"Yes…"

There were two key phrases in this letter.

Silviana mentioned *meeting beneath the full moon* and *being blessed by the moon*.

The full moon symbolized the mating season, and a moon blessing meant pregnancy.

If one was to read between the lines, she was clearly declaring that she was currently in heat and wanted to be impregnated with Bash's child.

This was an invitation to mate!

There could be no doubt about it. That was what the magazine said after all.

"Boss, let me check again."

"Right."

"The magazine says that you shouldn't go getting cocky just because a beastkin woman is in heat. The likelihood of securing a bride is a lot higher in this scenario, but many still report being rejected at this stage. You must bear that in mind."

"Of course."

"Also…"

Then Zell suddenly looked at the last page of the magazine.

One disturbing thing was written there…

…but there's no point in worrying about that now.

And so Zell deliberately ignored it.

The gist of it was something like... Let's put this in terms of military operations. Suppose that a tremendously strong opponent, much like Bash himself, should appear. His entire army might scatter.

One had to be aware of such a possibility, but it was pointless for those without countermeasures in place to worry about it.

Even Bash was aware of the possibility the final page of the magazine had mentioned.

But he would continue to fight bravely, even when confronted by a formidable opponent against whom victory seemed slim.

"Then let's go over everything by tomorrow! First, let's start from page twenty-two. 'Even in a spicy atmosphere, you must never forget your manners! Beastkin Etiquette 101'!"

"Right!"

Bash would prepare as well as he could for battle.

That was all the two of them could do.

■

Lycaon Palace lay at the center of the beastkin capital, Lycant.

There were members of almost every race in attendance.

Beastkin, humans, elves, dwarves.

Lizardmen, succubi, harpies, ogres, fairies, and even demons.

The only ones who hadn't been invited were the orcs.

However, there was one orc present, despite the supposed lack of an invitation. And he had an incredibly easygoing expression on his face.

But Bash had been sent an invitation. And he arrived with it firmly in hand.

"Hmm. So even the Orc Hero is here."

"I suppose the beastkin couldn't kick out an orc."

"Well, of course not. Regular orcs, sure. But this one is an Orc *Hero*."

"I'd like to say hello, but..."

"Mmm..."

"But is it really okay to approach an Orc Hero for conversation...?"

Few guests actually spoke to Bash.

Members of the Coalition of Seven seemed especially fidgety while catching glimpses of Bash from afar.

Bash's military achievements were so notable that even the elite of each country shied away from him.

Or maybe they shied away specifically *because* they were the elite.

If this had been a tavern on the outskirts of town, or right after an arena battle, they would no doubt have gleefully approached Bash and badgered him about his war victories.

But this was not the time nor the place.

This was the beastkin royal palace. The wedding venue of Innuella, the third-born beastkin princess.

All in attendance were there as diplomatic representatives of their respective countries. They could not afford to get starry-eyed over Bash right now.

Much of the beastkin royal family hated orcs after all.

Getting along with an orc at a beastkin wedding could invite reproach.

"Hmm? Who is that?"

A figure was approaching Bash.

A small figure, accompanied by a companion, who came and stood next to Bash.

"Hmm?"

It was an elf.

An elf whom all knew.

And tension rose in the air among those who knew the history between the elves and the orcs.

"Huh? Ho! *Gurgle burgle!*"

An odd sound issued from the elf.

On closer inspection, the elf's mouth was filled with something.

The table at the venue was crowded with dishes, and the elf was gobbling them up, one after another.

The elf's cheeks puffed out like a squirrel's.

How terribly greedy.

However, there were many elves who knew of the Great Famine four hundred years ago.

During that period, elves often had to go without food for weeks at a time. If they didn't eat everything they could whenever food was available, they would have surely starved to death.

...But today, there was only one living elf who had experienced the famine firsthand.

"That looks like Thunder Sonia."

"...I didn't catch a word of that, Boss. What's she doing, exactly?"

"She appears to be eating."

The elf, Thunder Sonia, mumbled rapidly as she rolled her eyes and chewed.

The elf woman by her side wiped Thunder Sonia's mouth and brushed the crumbs from her clothes.

Apparently, Thunder Sonia hadn't approached Bash on purpose. She was just working her way around the tables and had ended up near him by chance.

"Mmm..."

The sight of the elf woman beside Thunder Sonia made Bash's heart race.

He had his sights set on another woman at the moment, but elves were Bash's type, and he couldn't control his wandering eye.

"...Oh, it's the Orc Hero Bash!"

The elf woman was also very beautiful, exactly Bash's taste.

On her head, however...there rested a hair ornament in the shape of a small white flower.

A silver clasp with small white gems...

...representing a white flower.

And this convinced Bash that the woman was married.

But what Bash *didn't* know was that this particular hair ornament was made in the shape of a flower known as a snowdrop.

In the language of flowers, a snowdrop was code for *"I wish for your death."*

It was the emblem of the elf army assassination unit.

"...Wh-what?"

She looked at Bash, her face stiffening.

Her hand was inside her clothes, and she was clutching a dagger, her stance tense and ready.

If the orc made one wrong move, she would fight... She wasn't confident that she could win against Bash, however, so she was quite panicked.

"Hey, don't stare at my assistant like that. I understand, you're wary around a member of the assassin squad. But the war is over, got it? Anyway, the other day, this one caused a bit of trouble, so I'm keeping her on probation right now. I won't let you get your paws on her."

At Thunder Sonia's words, Bash averted his gaze.

He had no intention of pursuing a married woman anyway.

"It's been a long time, Lord Bash."

"Indeed. Our last meeting was in the Shiwanashi Forest, yes?"

"Mm-hmm. See, I'm here to celebrate my... I guess he's kinda like my nephew? Aconitum, I mean. He's the guy you helped out back at the Shiwanashi Forest, remember? At first, I thought I'd hide my identity, too. I didn't want too much of a fuss caused over me. But as I said, there was a bit of an incident, and I got found out right away. That nephew of mine... He was all, 'Thunder Sonia, you don't need to go to such lengths. Just hang out and enjoy yourself.' He could have been a bit more appreciative! After all the times I've wiped his ass! And I mean that literally! I used to change his diapers when he was a baby! Honestly..."

"...I see."

"Anyway, I'm surprised to see you here as well. Now, don't take that the wrong way. I actually think it makes perfect sense for you to be here. The six princesses might not be too pleased, though. Still, you were the last warrior to fight against the Hero Leto. Your being here must strike a nerve."

Bash was perplexed.

Thunder Sonia talked to him as if he were an old friend, but he didn't remember ever being this friendly with her.

He had proposed to her, yes. But she'd turned him down. He had expected that their relationship would end then and there.

Or did all elf women try to maintain a friendly relationship with the men who'd proposed to them?

Either way, Bash didn't really mind.

Thunder Sonia had rejected him, yes, but her face was still nice to look at.

She was as beautiful as ever, cute, and adorable. So cute, in fact, that if only Bash could have cast off his virginity with her, he would have been happy to never mate with another woman for the rest of his life.

He didn't mind chatting with a beauty like her at all.

Still, he was a little taken aback. The Thunder Sonia he'd met hadn't spoken this eloquently.

"...Huh. I had no idea she was such a chatterbox, Boss."

"I know, it's surprising. She always seemed quite grumpy."

"Hey, I can hear you two, you know. But whatevs. It's a happy day for me, too. I guess it's made me extra talkative, you know?"

Thunder Sonia smiled at the elf woman beside her, Bougainvillea. But Bougainvillea seemed confused.

The Thunder Sonia she knew was always blabbering away.

If anything, she was alarmed that Thunder Sonia would be chatting to this Bash with her usual frankness.

"Um, Thunder Sonia, are you close with this man, Lord Bash?"

"Hmm? No, I wouldn't say we're all that close. But, like, the war's over. I have no reason *not* to be friendly to him, y'know? It's best if we all get along from now on, isn't it?"

Thunder Sonia grinned and whacked Bash on the arm.

The casual contact set a fire burning in Bash's virgin loins.

If she hadn't turned him down once, or if he hadn't already been deeply invested in another woman, he might have jumped ship to team Thunder Sonia then and there.

A simple touch was enough to make him burn with yearning. A virgin was such a pitiful creature.

"..."

But Bash remained stalwart.

His target was not Thunder Sonia, but another.

He couldn't afford to lose sight of his goal and get distracted by a woman he had already struck out with.

But her touch had rendered him speechless. Thunder Sonia's hand was cool and soft. He wanted her to touch him more. He wanted to talk to her more. Much, much more.

But he could not stay.

Bash needed to leave the ceremonies at the appropriate time and go to Silviana. Awaiting him was none other than the loss of his virginity, in the form of Silviana's lush body.

...Still, he yearned for Thunder Sonia to touch him again.

A beautiful woman in the hand is worth two in the bush... Er, the forest.

He wanted to go. He wanted to stay.

With such conflicting feelings tugging him in both directions, Bash grimaced.

Seeing that, Bougainvillea hurriedly lowered her head.

"I... I'm so sorry! Thunder Sonia has caused offense!"

"Wh-whaddaya mean, 'offense'? I just tapped him on the shoulder a little bit. I didn't even hit him that hard... Unless you're talking about that business back at the Shiwanashi Forest? All right, my bad. Perhaps I was a bit harsh. But it couldn't be helped. You understand, right?"

"No. There is no need to apologize."

Bash didn't really understand what she was apologizing for, and even if an explanation had been given, he probably wouldn't have understood that, either. But he shook his head anyway.

"Come to think of it, it seems like you had a tough time the other day, too. You were harangued by the six princesses and all. If they bother you again, you come and tell me. I'll give 'em a talking-to. Just leave it to me, okay? I may be tiny, but I'm mighty as well."

Thunder Sonia puffed out her small chest.

Bash's gaze was nailed to that modest yet alluring bust, and his jaw fell slack.

It gave the impression that Bash was merely showing a wry response to Thunder Sonia's boasting.

Attendees nearby looked on with envious gazes, muttering, "Thunder Sonia is lucky to be enjoying a chat with Lord Bash."

The venue was beginning to fill with an indescribable, but not especially negative, atmosphere.

"Anyway, if they get upset again, just tell the whole story about the time when you fought the Hero Leto. It may be a little late in the day, but I'm sure they'll appreciate getting some closure..."

Just as Thunder Sonia was making this suggestion, a clamor rose from the back of the venue.

"Oh, looks like it's speech time."

"Speech? Princess Innuella's?"

"Yeah. Looks like Aconitum and the Queen will be giving speeches, too."

Princess Innuella's speech was about to begin.

That fact brought Bash to his senses.

The letter said, *Meet me beneath the Sacred Tree when Innuella's speech begins.*

He couldn't hang around here chitchatting.

"Actually, I also helped with the drafting of the Queen's speech. I mean, it was no big deal, but Leona said she was so worried, and I just gave her a few pointers. I've given plenty of important speeches in my time, so something like this is just..."

"Please excuse me."

"Oh, hey, where are you going? The speeches are about to begin! I mean, you don't *have* to tell me, but— Ah, of course, the bathroom! Were you holding it in this whole time? I'm so sorry! Just be back in time for the toasts, okay?"

Bash quickly started walking toward the Sacred Tree that towered high beyond the building.

After all, he couldn't keep a lady waiting.

9

The Seed of the Sacred Tree

Access to the beastkin's Sacred Tree was prohibited.

However, that rule didn't apply to the royal family. Those of royal blood didn't need permission.

Silviana had come to the Sacred Tree accompanied by a shrouded Carrot. They passed a few guards along the way, but the guards didn't pay them any mind.

Currently, Silviana was watching as Carrot prayed before the Sacred Tree.

It was the first time she'd ever seen a succubus pray.

The general impression of succubi was that they were wild and lascivious.

...And that was a pretty accurate assumption.

Typically, in the presence of an eye-catching man, a succubus's cheeks would flush, both mouths would water, and she would be all over him in seconds.

From the point of view of other races, they appeared to be extremely slovenly, uncouth, and even obscene.

It would seem succubus faith painted an entirely different picture, however.

Carrot knelt down before the Sacred Tree Silviana had guided her to, took off her stifling robe, and kissed its large trunk.

It was different from the beastkin way of praying.

If a beastkin priest saw this, they might have branded Carrot a heretic and ordered her to leave. But she looked so pure and pious in the moment, it was hard to believe she was really a member of the succubus race.

There was no special reason why only the royal family was allowed to approach the Sacred Tree without permission. It was simply to prevent treacherous people from damaging or cutting down the Sacred Tree.

But there didn't seem to be any cause for concern with Carrot.

Her respect for the Sacred Tree was evident, and her prayers were earnest.

It seemed to Silviana that Carrot had truly approached her in order to offer her prayers to the tree.

It had no doubt been a long time since she'd prayed, so it would probably take her a while. In all honesty, Silviana wanted her to finish up quickly so she could wait for Bash.

And just as she was thinking that, Carrot stood up.

"Are you done?"

"Yes, that should do it. You have my thanks."

However, when Carrot turned around, there was something unfamiliar in her hand.

A translucent red sphere. She hadn't been carrying that earlier...

"What's that?"

"None of your business."

Carrot's expression when she spoke those words to Silviana seemed almost... mocking.

"...What's with that face?"

"What face?"

"That face you just made. It was rather unpleasant."

"Ah-ha-ha, apologies. That's just how my face looks."

"It doesn't matter what kind of face you have, but since your wish was granted, you'd better hold up your end of the bargain and help me out as well."

"Hee-hee-hee. Yes, of course. I have no doubt he'll arrive soon."

Carrot looked at the entrance of the path to the Sacred Tree, laughing her bewitching laugh.

There came a large shadow. A shadow too big to be that of a human or beastkin.

A shadow smaller than an ogre.

It belonged to an orc.

But Silviana noticed something.

Something was wrong. This orc appeared to be slightly larger than Bash. Bash was one size larger than most beastkin, basically a giant in their eyes.

But this orc was one size bigger again than even Bash.

And there was something strange about it.

Its color. This orc looked more bluish than Bash did.

Bash's skin was green, the color of the common orc.

This wasn't Bash, then. This was someone else.

"Carrot..."

Silviana turned around.

However, Carrot simply continued to laugh.

"...What's going on?"

Silviana's mind filled with anxiety.

A shiver down her spine told her something was wrong.

"...!"

Silviana immediately tried to run.

But she didn't get far. Before she realized what was happening, her face was being slammed into the ground.

"Oh dear, what a fuss...," said Carrot.

Silviana realized that Carrot had kicked her legs out from under her. Now she was pulling her arms around her back, straddling her legs.

"What...?! Let go!"

"All I'm doing is sitting on you. You ought to be able to shake me off. Clearly someone hasn't been exercising."

"Somebody, help! Guards! *Guards!*"

"Um, hello? No one's coming. I charmed all the guards we passed along the way."

Silviana jerked and struggled as Carrot mocked her from above, but her elbow joints were completely locked.

Silviana groaned and kicked her legs frantically.

"But I fulfilled your wish!"

"Yeah, thanks to you, I was able to get close to the Sacred Tree. I was even able to get my little servant here access as well. And check *this* out! I extracted the seed of the Sacred Tree easy peasy."

Carrot tossed the red sphere around like a beanbag, still smiling her bewitching smile.

"You betrayed me?!"

"Yes, you idiot. You're not that bright, are you…?"

Silviana's face burned crimson over being called an idiot and then gradually turned blue.

She had truly believed she had control over the situation.

She thought she'd chosen the best possible method to take down Bash.

"Aw, don't beat yourself up. I'm Carrot the Breathstealer after all. See, my charm is so good it even steals the breath of women."

"…!"

"It's not as effective as when I cast it on a man, to be sure, but it's enough to amplify your desires, make you lose your reason, and leave your heart vulnerable. It's not *all* because you're stupid. So don't blame yourself too much."

Charm magic that also worked on women.

Such a thing wasn't supposed to exist.

Silviana's mind was screaming that this was impossible. But if she'd been in her right mind, she would have been able to think more rationally.

In order to prevent this kind of situation from happening, she should have at least taken the essential safety precautions.

She knew she had a tendency to act without thinking. She'd also known, instinctively, that Carrot was the devious type.

"What are you going to do with me?!"

"Not a whole lot, really. I'm just gonna sit here and watch you die…"

"Guh…!"

Silviana went berserk.

But she was unable to free herself.

The blue orc now stood above her…with hollow eyes and drool dripping from his mouth.

"Stop! Let go!"

"But you know, I think I've changed my mind. Simply watching you die would be too boring."

"What? You mean…?"

"Hee-hee-hee."

Carrot's words made all the blood drain from Silviana's face.

Was she going to let this blue orc defile her?

Unable to take revenge on Bash, her body desecrated by some strange orc... She would be subjected to the worst possible humiliation and then beheaded.

It was no way to die.

"Why are you doing this?! What did I ever do to you?!"

"Lord Bash... The Orc Hero...is our guardian angel. But it's not just we succubi who have cause to worship him. Every race in the Coalition of Seven has been saved by him at least once. A little strumpet like you is not a good enough match for him. Do you understand?"

Gradually, Carrot's voice changed.

It morphed into a low, sharp, muffled voice filled with hate.

"You treated him so callously and even tried to deceive him. I wasn't about to let you get away with that. A clean death is too good for the likes of you. You'll get the punishment you deserve. A punishment that'll make you wish you were already dead."

Silviana finally realized that she had stepped on the tiger's tail.

The Orc Hero Bash.

A demon of the battlefield, the subject of decorated war anecdotes from all over the world, a man who had many nicknames, who was feared and respected by anyone wise in years and strong of body.

By everyone.

Fierce men and women of all races feared and revered him.

He had fought on every battlefield. Been victorious. And helped many along the way.

Just as all the beastkin adored the Hero Leto, all the warriors of the Coalition of Seven adored Bash.

Succubi were no exception.

"But Lord Bash, he's really something, isn't he? Even though he found himself in a foreign land and dared to go on a date with a foreign princess, he was able to properly comport himself like a gentleman. Dating etiquette may be written about in all the magazines now, but the orcs have never had a culture of dating or romancing. No doubt he studied up, anticipating that something like this would happen. He is so different from most orcs. He's... He's a scholar."

Carrot blushed, speaking as if enraptured.

Silviana was horrified, her eyes flicking back and forth.

She needed to get out of this situation somehow.

But she couldn't free herself.

Carrot the Breathstealer was one of the veteran warriors who'd made a name for themselves in the war. At first glance, she seemed like a common floozy, but her power was undeniable. In terms of strength, there was simply no comparison between her and Silviana. Even if she was able to wriggle free, Silviana would not have the means to deal with the strong blue orc standing by Carrot's side.

All she could do was run her mouth.

"Are you going to have me raped and killed just for that?! Th-that will make Bash furious, you know!"

"How so?"

"He was careful not to lay a hand on me! He was careful not to spark any discord between the beastkin and the orcs. But what you're doing... It flies in the face of all his effort!"

"Ah..."

"That's right! I-if you kill me, there will be a war! All will perish! Orcs and succubi both!"

"What are you talking about? That's what you want, isn't it? ...But you're right about one thing. Lord Bash probably won't be very happy about this..."

"Good, we're on the same page. So get off me! Let me go!"

Silviana was grinning inside.

She had to do her best not to smirk.

The moment she was released, she would run to the wedding venue and spill everything. She'd tell everyone how she was trapped by a succubus, on the verge of being violated by an orc.

"But Lord Bash *is* an orc, you know. If I explain everything to him, I'm sure he'll side with me. I mean, how angry do you imagine an orc would be to find out he was almost tricked by a lying bitch like you?"

"Th-that's assuming he'd believe you!"

"Oh, he will. Our friendship goes all the way back to the war."

Carrot blushed coyly, lifting the red sphere.

"Besides, getting Lord Bash on my side isn't the main reason I'm here."

The red sphere.

Something akin to a holy aura was emanating from it.

Come to think of it, Carrot didn't have that before she'd started smooching the Sacred Tree.

Perhaps it was something she'd taken from the tree itself?

"...!"

The thought horrified Silviana.

She appeared to have made an irreparable mistake.

She'd been willing to do whatever it took to achieve her goal, but she'd ended up jeopardizing something much more precious than her own pride.

"This is the seed of the Sacred Tree, and it has tremendous power. Normally, it can only be harvested when the Sacred Tree is dug up and replaced, but with a succubus energy drain, you see..."

"The seed of the Sacred Tree...? What do you want with that?"

"It's actually a secret, but I don't mind telling you."

Carrot put her mouth to Silviana's ear and whispered.

As if she were making cozy pillow talk in bed. As if she were whispering sweet nothings to her soon-to-be victim.

"...I'm going to resurrect Lord Geddigs."

The Demon Lord Geddigs.

Because of him, the Alliance of Four almost fell apart. With him gone, the Coalition of Seven was finally defeated. His death had brought the war to an end.

His was the final sacrifice to the god of war.

He had been the most vicious, the most evil, and the most hated man across the thousands of years of war.

If he was to be resurrected...

"If you do that...the entire world will be..."

Silviana remembered when she was young...when she had to live in fear of everything.

She remembered screams echoing in the darkness. She remembered the maid who greeted her in the morning and had vanished the next night.

But one day, the nightmare ended.

With the help of the elves and the humans, and the struggle of the Hero Leto, the beastkin race recovered.

Ever since then, Silviana had enjoyed a lifestyle befitting a beastkin princess.

But now her days of happiness seemed numbered.

This time around, no one would be able to defeat the Demon Lord Geddigs. There was no way that great and terrible man would repeat the same mistake.

This time, the beastkin race would perish. Cornered, as they were then, but with no hope of help this time. They would never again be able to rebuild their race.

Because the Hero Leto was no more.

"Don't worry. I'll let you witness the state of the new world from a *very special* seat. You'll be the wife of an orc, the very race you hate the most..."

"You... You plan to give me to...to Bash?"

"What are you talking about? There's no way a vicious, vindictive woman like you would be suitable for Lord Bash!"

Carrot's eyes glowed red, and the blue orc stirred.

"Hee-hee, what a good mistress I am. To be able to reward my faithful servant with such a pretty wife! ...Gagan. You may take her."

Silviana was suddenly released, and she was able to scramble to her feet. But it was too soon to hope. The orc threw himself on her, knocking her to the ground.

His eyes were hollow and empty, but his crotch was greatly swollen.

As if to hint at Silviana's fate.

"No! Let me go! Don't!"

"Hee-hee-hee, Gagan looks so happy. Come to think of it, before I made him my servant, he said it was his dream to violate a princess and have her give birth to many babies... Beastkin have multiple young per birth, don't they? See that you give him lots of strong children. Make his dreams come true."

"Somebody, somebody, please help me!"

"There's no one around to hear you. This is the back of the royal palace, and all the guards around here have become my servants. And Lord Bash won't be here anytime soon. Unless... Hey, are you a virgin? Hmm, maybe I *should* have saved you for him after all. Well, no matter. I'm sure he enjoyed a fair number of virgin princesses during the war."

"Someone! Someone, please!"

"Oh, quit screaming. No one's coming."

Carrot chuckled, and then...

"I wouldn't be so sure about that."

Those words came from the forest path.

Carrot, Silviana, and the blue orc known as Gagan all looked up.

A man was standing at the entrance.

Carrot smiled as if she had been anticipating him.

"Oh, Lord Bash, you're early! Allow me to explain the situation..."

But then she trailed off.

The man wore a mask shaped like a woman's face and clutched a musical instrument.

His skin was pale, and his body was small...like a human's.

In fact, he *was* human.

""...Who are you?""

Carrot's and Silviana's voices sounded in unison.

The man strummed his instrument.

"The emissary of love and peace, Errol, has arrived."

Twaaang! ...He played an especially sour note.

10
The Cry of the Succubus

A deadpan silence hung in the air following the man's sudden appearance.

Carrot, for one, seemed distinctly unimpressed.

"...Huh? Are you the jester they booked for the ceremony? This isn't the wedding venue, you know?"

"I may appear a tad wild and crazy to some, but I am no jester."

Errol cleared his throat loudly, let out an "ahh-ahh" sound, and then *twang*ed his instrument again.

A noise like a pig's dying squeal issued forth.

The two women braced themselves, wondering if he was about to perform a troubadour act, but when he spoke, the words were not lyrics.

"Carrot the Breathstealer, I have been pursuing you."

"Huh? What are you, some kind of crazy fan? I encounter them from time to time, you know... Losers desperate to be consumed by me..."

"I heard that a faction hell-bent on reviving Geddigs was planning to act during the wedding ceremony. I've been pursuing you for a long time. Had I not realized a charm spell had been cast in the vicinity of the Sacred Tree, I might not have been able to corner you... I'm glad I made it in time."

"...Who are you, really?"

Carrot stepped backward, toward Silviana, her eyes narrowed.

Errol took a step forward.

"Carrot. As a Hero of the succubi, you ought to be in a position of renown within your own country."

"Hmph. You didn't answer my question. Still, I like a man who's persistent."

"Why would you want to restore Geddigs? Why destroy an era of peace and revive an era of turmoil?"

Hearing that, Carrot, who'd been smiling placidly, suddenly froze.

"Peace? Did you say 'peace'?"

Carrot snorted and held out an arm, posing.

Errol's eyes drank in the sight of Carrot's slender limbs.

It really was a sensational outfit. Any human male would be attracted to her, if they didn't know she was a succubus, that is.

"Does this outfit look good on me?"

"Oh yes. It's...bewitching."

"Isn't it? I like it, too. But...have you heard of this? The Treaty of Runius, Article Sixteen."

It was a well-known treaty.

"...Succubi must not expose their skin in other countries."

"Right. Thanks to that law, we've been forbidden from wearing our favorite clothes."

"But that law should only prohibit exposing the, um, intimate areas."

"Oh? And where exactly is that stipulated? *Skin*, it says! And skin is skin! Chest, shoulders, arms, back, legs, fingers, all skin! I even have to hide my hair and my face when I travel to other countries! Now then! The Treaty of Runius, Article Seventeen!"

"...A succubus must not seduce a man in public."

"Oh, you know what's weird about that? Even saying hello is apparently too much of a temptation!"

"..."

"We succubi are basically forbidden from speaking with men of different races in public!"

Carrot's voice gradually grew louder.

Before long, she was screaming.

"My people are starving! It's not just the old and young! Succubi born after the war are also dying because they can't get enough to eat! That's right! Because *you* people impose all these restrictions on our ability to feed!"

"That's because you succubi drained those war criminals to death one year after the war."

"We didn't kill them for the fun of it! We were starving! We couldn't find enough food on our own because of the new rules! And none of your countries gave us any support!"

"That's because no country would knowingly send people to their deaths."

"Lies!! You used to send us criminals! Exiles banished from your lands! You didn't care if *those* people lived or died!"

"..."

"Even if we endured the current situation, and followed the rules that were decided unilaterally, we would still face hatred and discrimination, simply for the crime of being succubi!"

"..."

"You call this *peace*?! Your peace seems terribly skewed in favor of the cultures of the Alliance of Four! Succubi are now teetering on the brink of extinction!"

"I understand. I will speak to the top brass and see if we can send a support delegation to your land to—"

"Give me a break!"

Carrot's shrieks ripped through the air around the Sacred Tree.

Errol was speechless.

There were tears pooling in the succubus's eyes.

"I've traveled all over the world in the past year. To entreat the people of each land, in the hopes that they might come to understand our plight, if only a little. I bent the knee and begged! But...you know what, human? —Or Errol, or whatever your name is... Do you know what happened when I went to your land? Do you know how I was treated?"

Errol didn't answer. He had no idea. He'd known nothing of the succubus's plight.

What he did know was that both humans and elves hated the succubi. The hatred from the women of these races was especially vitriolic.

In that way, they were the natural ally of the orcs.

Succubi were forbidden from speaking to men in public.

The top brass of each country had assigned officers to deal with the succubi.

And the person in charge on the human side was a woman who was famous for hating succubi.

Errol didn't know what Carrot had been told or how she had been treated.

However, there was a significant possibility that her rights and dignity had not been protected.

"I'm sorry about that. I'll apologize on behalf of the woman in charge."

"Oh, whatever. You won't fill our empty stomachs by bowing your heads. Besides, it's not just *your* country. The dwarves were a bit more sympathetic, but the elves were just as bad as the humans... And the beastkin are brutes, too!"

Carrot placed her hand on Silviana's head as she lay pinned by the blue orc.

Despite their slender arms, succubi could use magic to strengthen their bodies at will.

She could have crushed Silviana's skull with minimal effort.

"I wanted to pray before the Sacred Tree. So first I went straight to the people in charge to make my request, you know? I said, 'I'm a succubus who believes in the god of the hunt. Please, let me pray to the Sacred Tree, just once.' I begged...and what do you think they said?"

Carrot's fingers went white as her grip strength increased.

"'A filthy race like yours, worshipping the god of the hunt? You will only make a mockery of that which is holy.' So you see?! Succubi are even denied their faith!"

"Stop!!" screamed Errol.

"...Don't worry, I won't kill her. Not yet."

Silviana's head remained uncrushed.

"I understand the situation you succubi are in. I will take action immediately, so please..."

"Ah-ha-ha! It's already too late! I don't have time to indulge your wishful thinking and empty promises! But since you're so willing to help, how about you come and visit the land of the succubi? We'll be *real* nice to you, if you know what I mean!"

"I'm sorry, I can't do that. I have my own duties. But I'll do something. I promise. I may be a bit late in the day, and this may sound like lip service, but I'm serious. I'm aiming for world peace, you see."

"If you had told me that a year ago, I might have willingly become your mistress, but...it's too late."

After saying that, Carrot let go of Silviana's head and stepped on her back again.

"The time for talk is over."

"And what will you do once she's been victimized? Do you really think you can escape from here?" asked Errol.

"It'll be easy enough to flee. I'll just walk out the door with my head held high."

"You think I'm going to let you do that?"

"Oh my, you plan to stop me? I'll get past you by force if need be."

"You really think you can take me?"

"Hah... Gagan, get this arrogant boy out of here."

The blue orc moved on Carrot's command.

Raising his ax, he advanced upon Errol.

Gagan was known as the Thunderous Roar.

He was a veteran warrior who cut across the battlefield faster than any other.

Even though he wasn't a mage, his striking blue skin lowered the temperature of anything it touched.

He was a graceful orc, with strong cold resistance as well as strong fire resistance.

He was one of the eight battalion commanders who had survived until the end of the war.

"Yes, it's a pity."

Errol brought a hand to the sword on his waist.

Just then, flames rose from the blade. The rags that covered the sword burned away, revealing its true form.

"...That sword!" Carrot gasped.

There were none who would not recognize it.

A sun pattern was engraved on the golden handle, and a red gem was embedded in its center.

The blade shone silvery white, and the heat haze wrapped all around it. Its beauty, its divine majesty, captivated the eyes of all who saw it.

The name of the sword was Sun.

The Sun Sword. One of the sacred objects of the human royal family.

Its slashing blow incinerated everything it touched and brought certain victory to the wielder.

"Let me give you my name again..."

Yes, his true name was not Errol, for he wielded the Sun Sword.

In that moment, the world changed. The clouds obscuring the sky cleared in an instant.

Rays of sunlight pierced the gloom.

Errol removed his mask. What lay beneath was a human face, a pristine face.

A slender face with slanted eyes. His flawless beauty indicated that no sword had ever touched that face on the battlefield.

Then he spoke his name aloud.

"My name is Nazar Liscia Gainius Grandolius! I am the second-born prince of the human royal family and the heir to the Sun Sword!"

Nazar. The Human Prince, Nazar.

He had another name: the Heaven-Sent Prince.

He was the strongest human swordsman, a Hero, and the one who had dealt the killing blow to Demon Lord Geddigs.

His path was illuminated by the sun.

"And so I will crush your ambitions and bring true peace to this world!"

"No! Get back, Gagan!"

But Carrot's warning came too late.

It wouldn't have been too late against a lesser opponent, perhaps. Gagan was an excellent warrior. He might have been able to retreat.

But his opponent was Nazar, and Nazar held the Sun Sword.

As ordered, Gagan took a backstep and wound up for the attack.

Only the right half of his body moved back, though. The left half of his body remained in place.

The huge body of the blue orc was split vertically in two.

Flames enveloped his two halves as they lost their balance and began to fall.

The flames burned the wounds in an instant and charred the body of the blue orc. When the two halves collapsed, there was no one who could tell that the owner of the body had ever had blue skin.

"...Gagan!"

Carrot's cry was a pained wail.

The orc did not reply. Unless one had extremely high physical and magical resistance, a single blow from the Sun Sword would result in certain death. The sword's power was so absolute, even recovery or resurrection magic was useless against it.

This was the weapon that had felled the Demon Lord Geddigs.

"...Surrender, Carrot. I'll see you're treated fairly."

"..."

Carrot did not answer.

Instead, with a detached expression on her face, Carrot planted a heel on Silviana, who was trying to escape.

"There's no way I'm going to surrender."

"Do you still intend to fight, even knowing the true identity of your opponent?"

"Well, I was surprised to learn that Errol was actually the prince, but...there's no reason for me to run away. You know that all too well, don't you?"

"...No, I don't believe I follow."

"You act confident, but you're trembling inside, right? There's no kind, strong older woman coming to save you... Not like back then."

"...I'm stronger than I was then."

As he spoke, Nazar lifted his sword. Dropping into an attack stance, he took a step forward...

Carrot's eyes glowed red.

"...!"

Nazar froze.

"The... The charm!"

"Wow, amazing magical resistance. I really went all out on you just now, too."

"I was born fully confident in my magic resistance..."

His tone was light, but Nazar was unable to move.

On the contrary, his expression was screwed-up, distorted in agony, and globules of sweat beaded his forehead.

"Yeah, it's a shock that Gagan died, but I'll just use the Human Prince Nazar instead. If you think about it, I'm making out like a bandit here."

"...Do you really think I'll fall into your clutches so easily?"

A human male against a succubus was the most one-sided battle on paper.

And against the Breathstealer, a person's chance of victory was generally no greater than 5 percent no matter who they were.

"Oh, you'll fall. There's no man alive who can resist my charm."

Carrot stared harder.

Immediately, Nazar's Sun Sword increased in brilliance. At the same time, the jewels, bracelets, and shoes around Nazar's neck also began to glow.

Carrot's red light was deflected, driven back.

"How much resistance equipment are you wearing...? You're geared to the teeth. Do humans really need all that? I thought you were confident in your skills."

"...I thought I might run into a situation like this."

Nazar did not let go of his sword, even though his face registered pain and struggle.

If Carrot were to approach and attempt to finish him off, or slip past him toward the exit, he would summon his strength and slash with all his might.

Carrot wasn't confident she could dodge that kind of blow.

If it was so easily avoidable, then this prince would have lost his life in the war long ago.

However, Nazar wasn't confident enough of victory to go charging in and attacking outright.

Time passed as they remained locked in place.

"It's a stalemate, then. Hmm, that's not ideal."

There was no impatience in Nazar's expression when he said that.

It would be troublesome if Silviana got killed, yes. But the longer they remained in this situation, the more likely it was that the guests at the wedding venue would stumble across it and get involved.

There were many guests present with sharp intuition... Not to mention, Thunder Sonia was also in attendance.

Thunder Sonia was Carrot's natural enemy.

During the war, Nazar had heard that each time Thunder Sonia and Carrot fought, Thunder Sonia claimed victory by a wide margin.

If Nazar could stall long enough, his victory was assured. Realizing this, he decided to bide his time.

"I see, you're thinking that if you buy as much time as you can, Thunder Sonia will notice and come with reinforcements..."

Carrot laughed.

"But you know, the next person to stumble across our path might not be on *your* side."

The moment Carrot said that, Nazar sensed a presence approaching from behind.

An overwhelming presence.

With each step the person took, fear swelled in his chest. It was like being stalked by a predator ten times Nazar's own size.

It came closer, step by step.

And it was moving quickly. It was light on its feet, and swift, as if impatient to close in on its prey.

The tension in the air rose to a fever pitch.

Except for Silviana, everyone present knew those footsteps well, that overwhelming presence.

The face would come into view any second...

"Ah, Boss. Here she is."

It was a fairy who popped into view.

For a moment, everyone was confused.

A fairy?

But in the next moment, they all stiffened.

They knew that fairy.

Whenever *he* appeared, the fairy led the way, as a sort of scout. And the fairy was often caught. Thus, giving it the nickname of...

"Fake-Bait Zell."

If you took the bait...then *he* would appear.

"Right."

And slowly, *he* emerged.

Green skin, short for an orc but incredibly muscular.

That well-honed body was clothed in the formal attire of the beastkin, and although he wasn't carrying the indestructible greatsword that was his trademark, his overwhelming presence was undeniable.

It was the Orc Hero Bash.

"No way... Are you one of her allies, too...?" Nazar muttered as cold sweat trickled down his spine.

11

A Messenger of Peace

Nazar Gainius Grandolius.

The third son and second-born prince of the human royal Grandolius family. The strongest human swordsman, the Heaven-Sent Prince, who'd defeated the Demon Lord Geddigs.

He was a true hero.

His entire life was blessed with glory... Only, not really.

The very beginning of his life had been tinged with defeat.

Nazar had a sister.

Liscia Gainius Grandolius.

She was his twin sister and was extremely talented.

Nazar had lived in her shadow ever since he was a baby, even before he'd formed memories.

Nazar was born after Liscia.

It was his sister who fed from their mother first, who first started crawling on all fours, who first stood on two legs.

By the time the two began swinging the sword, a difference began to appear, one so clear that everyone could see it.

The swordplay, the speed of the feet, the academic ability.

Nazar couldn't beat his sister at anything.

However, Nazar was not without talent.

He fell short of his older sister by only a small margin, and if Liscia hadn't been born, Nazar would have become the strongest being in human history.

Nazar's grandfather, the Human King at the time, ordered Nazar's father to raise them equally.

He firmly believed these twins would change the course of the war.

That promise was upheld. Nazar and Liscia were raised the same and became the strongest twins alive.

Liscia inherited the most powerful object of the human royal family, the Thunder Sword, and Nazar inherited the Sun Sword.

The Cloudburst Princess and the Cloudbreak Prince.

Hearing those names made even the most famous enemy generals shudder.

It would be a lie to say that Nazar didn't have an inferiority complex.

However, the war situation at that time was so bad, there was no room for caring about such things.

Rather, it was reassuring to have such a strong warrior in the form of an older sister.

It wasn't like they were on bad terms. They were always together, eating the same things, seeing the same things, telling the same jokes, and laughing the same way.

Nazar knew everything about Liscia.

So there was no reason for him to hold any grudges against her.

But things wouldn't remain this way for long.

Liscia was always one step ahead of Nazar. She entered the battlefield one step before Nazar, defeated one more enemy than Nazar, and saved one more ally than Nazar.

She also died earlier than Nazar.

In order to allow their allies to escape the battlefield when the situation was beyond repair, she remained behind with a small number of death squad soldiers and did not return.

Her body was never recovered.

Everyone said that Liscia was so strong and capable, she must have escaped and was living somewhere else.

However, after that, the enemy army announced that they had killed the human princess Liscia, and as the morale of their enemies rose, the humans fell into despair.

Liscia had been, undoubtedly, the hope of all humans.

Nazar knew he would die on the next battlefield.

Because it had always been that way.

Although he was one step behind, there was nothing Liscia could do that he couldn't do.

There was nothing that ever happened to Liscia that didn't also happen to him.

So he was going to die. That much was certain.

With that mentality, he set out for his next battle.

And he survived. He defeated the Demon Lord Geddigs in the decisive battle of the Remium Plateau.

The battles that followed were like something out of a dream.

Victory after victory. There were a few defeats, but those didn't matter much.

At some point, Nazar began to gain fame as the human prince and hero who had killed Geddigs... Liscia's name had all but disappeared from people's memories.

Well, most would remember if they heard the name. *Oh yes. I forgot about her,* they would say.

No matter how great a hero someone might be, if they died and another hero appeared, they would become a relic of the past.

Take the Hero Leto, for example. If subsequent heroes had not come along to supersede him, he would have been remembered for a long time. But most heroes were only remembered because of the people who killed them, and most often, their names were only mentioned in bardsong and poetry.

But Nazar remembered.

He remembered the days when he and his sister used to talk. The absurd story she told the day before she died.

A story about a dream world that Nazar could not even imagine. He'd been spellbound.

A story about a world free from conflict, where all races would coexist.

So when the war turned completely in favor of the Alliance of Four, Nazar decided to do something else.

He made up his mind to make Liscia's dream come true.

He would bring peace to the world.

It was Nazar who proposed the idea of postwar peace before anyone else.

And from that day forward, Nazar went by the name Nazar Liscia Gainius Grandolius.

Because he was Nazar, but now he also bore the will of Liscia, the progenitor of world peace.

■   ■   ■

Three years had gone by.

Nazar had been working hard for world peace. He traveled around the world, plucking the buds of conflict wherever they sprouted. Spreading the word, in the name of Nazar.

However, the name of the Human Prince Nazar caused an unnecessary uproar.

There were those who capitalized on Nazar's efforts and used them as a way to make money. There were those who lurked in the shadows, unbeknownst to Nazar, and there were those who would ridicule and mock the prince and act as though he traveled to different countries just for fun.

Therefore, halfway through his travels, he assumed the identity of Errol, the emissary of love and peace.

Still, there were many times when he had to invoke the Nazar name.

The people would not follow a man named Errol. He could not gather much information, nor could he act effectively.

So he usually went about his days as Errol and only used the name Nazar when necessary.

Day and night, Nazar continued to work. Talking things out when he could and using force when he could not.

To be honest, he had to resort to force more often than not.

The Alliance of Four, which had won the war, preyed on the nations of the Coalition of Seven, and those in an advantageous position were often loath to relinquish said advantage. Aiming for perfect peace, Nazar tried to balance the scales and was ostracized by the humans in power because of it.

He knew the situation in each country was getting worse. Now he had to use the name Nazar to get any information out of anyone.

He endured a great many assassination attempts.

Those who hated Nazar had tried to kill him. Nazar had no choice but to take revenge against them.

But killing only brought about fresh problems.

The war was supposed to be over, but Nazar's hands were still stained with blood. He was beginning to lose sight of what peace even was. Originally, Nazar knew nothing but war. He had no idea what to do to get closer to peace. He was just blindly groping about in the dark.

And he was getting tired of feeling lost.

A part of him was on the verge of giving up on Liscia's dream.

Then a certain piece of information reached his ears.

"There are people out there who are trying to revive the Demon Lord Geddigs and reignite the war."

The Demon Lord Geddigs.

Nazar, who had actually fought him, knew the Demon Lord's strength all too well.

It wasn't his individual strength that was the issue, though. After all, many great and terrible individuals had been active throughout the long, long war.

The true threat of the revival of the Demon Lord Geddigs was all that would follow.

If Geddigs was resurrected and the war resumed, this time the Alliance of Four would crumble.

It was even possible that one or two races under the Coalition of Seven might be wiped out in their entirety.

The result would be an odd sort of peace. Under the rule of Geddigs, the world would become one.

But that wasn't the kind of peace anyone wanted.

The peace that Nazar Liscia Gainius Grandolius was aiming for was a world where all races could live in happiness.

Just as Liscia had talked about.

So Nazar was determined to stop the resurrection.

For that reason, even if a small-scale conflict occurred, he was willing to devote himself wholeheartedly to thwarting the enemy's schemes.

Even if he had to fight dirty, even if it was difficult to justify his actions in the name of peace.

He was confident that he could do it, no matter the cost.

■

Nazar was a human prince.

It was generally known that he was the strongest human swordsman. But even against him, there were some opponents who still had a slim chance of winning.

The first one was Carrot the Breathstealer.

He'd faced her three times during the war.

Nazar had been defeated all three times, saved by his older sister Liscia.

Liscia overwhelmed Carrot, and the two quickly retreated.

Liscia so greatly outmatched Carrot that she always held the advantage.

Liscia was stronger than Nazar, but only by a small margin.

Nazar probably could have won if he'd fought Carrot in a fair fight, but not when she used her charm. Nazar would never be able to win against that. It was like pitting a cat against a mouse.

So Nazar, and the human royal family, had been working out countermeasures against succubi for a long time.

They spent a long while strategizing so that in the event of a one-on-one fight, the odds would be more evenly balanced.

However...

"No way... Are you one of her allies, too...?"

The Orc Hero Bash.

Nazar had met him twice before.

The first time, Bash hadn't seemed like much of a threat. Then again, they hadn't actually fought. At the time, the human army was in the process of retreating, and Bash was but one of many threats.

There were many individuals of a higher threat level than Bash at that time.

It was later that he realized: *Back then, there was one green orc that was stronger than the others.*

He would never forget the second time.

It was immediately after the defeat of the Demon Lord Geddigs.

He had appeared, an overwhelming adversary dripping with the blood of his enemies.

Shortly after overthrowing the Demon Lord Geddigs, Nazar was badly wounded. Thunder Sonia was unconscious. Doradoradobanga was dead.

The only person who could still fight was the brave Leto, and even Leto was in critical condition.

That day, Nazar withdrew, and Leto died.

Later, he learned that the orc was a monster of many names.

He learned that he was the one who'd defeated the dragon in the decisive battle of the Remium Plateau.

Then. The interim period of years between the death of Geddigs and the official end of the war. Nazar heard many rumors of the orc and thought that he himself would have to settle the matter at some point. He wasn't sure if he could win, but he felt he had to make amends for retreating with Thunder Sonia slung over his shoulder back then.

But the war ended before that.

Nazar brought it to an end.

He participated in the peace talks with the orc country, stood near Bash as they listened to Lily the Blood Sprayer speak, and signed the agreement, all while Bash watched him.

At the time of their meeting, Bash appeared to be one of the most formidable orcs, a ferocious creature utterly devoid of peace.

However, that day, Nazar was convinced that the opportunity to fight Bash would never come again.

"Allies, you say...?"

But now, seeing Bash's terrifying face as he looked back and forth between Nazar and Carrot, Nazar had to dismiss that notion.

It was a tall order, to begin with.

Peace among all races and all that.

As Carrot had just said, the world in this era of "peace" continued to be a hostile environment for the losing nations.

While the influential people of the victorious nations were growing fat and prosperous, the races that were especially hated (even among the defeated nations) were weak and oppressed.

Those who were not satisfied with the current situation in their home countries went rogue, and the situation worsened each time they committed evil deeds in foreign countries.

Carrot tried it, but she had been thwarted.

If only Nazar had met her when she came to the human country, he might have been able to do something for her. The gesture might have been insignificant, but if he acted in his role as the famed Nazar, he might have been able to provide something in the way of food rations to the succubi.

However, there was no way the elites in human government would be so foolish as to bring a succubus to bother the famed Nazar. And so her grievances were silenced long before they could reach his ears.

Nazar had traveled the world, but he hadn't realized the succubus country was in such dire straits.

Nazar was not familiar with the current situation in the orc country, either.

Intel on the orcs, who stayed out of diplomatic matters, was scarcer even than intel on the succubi.

However, unbeknownst to Nazar, the Coalition of Seven was steadily dissolving.

Orcs were even worse at diplomacy than the succubi. No one would be surprised if the orcs were absorbed by another country. Gagan the Thunderous Roar was one of the vicious rogue orcs acting out of a sense of disillusionment.

Yes, even the honorable battalion commanders who'd survived the war were dissatisfied with the current state of the country. And so they absconded and went rogue.

To be honest, Nazar had been chilled to the bone when he'd heard news that Bash had embarked on a journey abroad.

It was presumed that the orc nation was on the verge of collapse, if even Orc Heroes were going rogue. But Nazar was relieved when he heard that Bash was eliminating rogue orcs and other troublemakers in each country he visited.

Nazar was pleased that the elves, the humans, and the dwarves understood the pride of the orcs and changed their perspective after encountering this Orc Hero.

It wasn't much, but it was surely a good thing that even those who'd held strong prejudices against the orcs had been able to reconsider and accept that orcs were proud warriors and people worthy of respect and common decency.

Nazar had been encouraged to hear Bash was working to restore the pride of the orcs.

Their methodology was a little different, but Nazar believed both he and Bash were ultimately working toward the same goal.

So when Bash appeared in the beastkin country, Nazar had helped him out.

He'd gotten him past the border and even guided him to the royal palace.

He knew the beastkin royal family held a grudge against the orcs for killing the Hero Leto. But if the beastkin could see that the orcs were earnestly celebrating the royal wedding, the beastkin people would slowly begin to change their minds. Nazar was confident that Bash could do this.

It would all work out just fine, he'd hoped.

However, Bash was kicked out of the wedding venue.

The beastkin princesses' hatred for orcs had never cooled.

Later, when he asked the princesses, "Why did you kick out the one known as Bash, a man who approached the beastkin race with such sincerity?" ...They'd snorted with reproach.

Anyone from the Alliance of Four could simply put on the right clothes and adopt the right attitude, they said.

They didn't even consider how much effort it would have taken for an orc to have come up with that.

When he heard that, Nazar thought about the pain and hardship Bash must have overcome on his journey.

How many heartless words had he endured, from the time he started his journey until now? How many tears of humiliation had he shed? He must have been discouraged so many times.

And after such harsh treatment...

...what would he do if he was invited to join a new war?

What would happen if he learned of the possibility of Geddigs's resurrection?

If there was another war, Bash would never have to experience such humiliation again...

If Nazar were Bash...he'd leap at the opportunity.

Nazar had heard from one of his war buddies, one of the human soldiers he trusted the most, how much importance the orcs placed on fighting and siring children.

In the event of war, the orcs would be able to regain their pride.

The orcs had agreed to peace because the war was a battle they could not win. But if Geddigs was resurrected, their victory would be all but assured.

"Hmm..."

Carrot the Breathstealer.

The Orc Hero Bash.

Humans were a race of wisdom and knowledge.

Even against opponents with superior physical strength, humans would work out countermeasures, prepare the right weapons and armor, act intelligently, and claim victory.

So they had no doubt made the necessary arrangements and brought the finest weapons here to the royal palace.

Nazar felt he could take on Carrot, or he could take on Bash.

But there was no way he could fight both at the same time.

Victory was impossible.

Even in a one-on-one match, the odds of winning were thin, but with Carrot's charm complicating things...

And in this situation, escape was next to impossible.

Even if Thunder Sonia herself came along and took on Carrot...would it be enough?

"Carrot."

Bash's voice sounded deep and calm.

No hesitation, as if he already knew what he wanted to say.

It was a voice that seemed to say, *Sorry I kept you waiting.*

"Yes. I've been waiting for you, Lord Bash."

Carrot's response was joyful.

There was no doubt that Bash and Carrot were in this together.

Without Nazar even knowing, Carrot had already recruited Bash.

Nazar made up his mind. Even if you can't win, there are times when you still have to resist.

As a prince, Nazar had always been protected. In order to save his life and secure victory for the humans, many soldiers had fought unwinnable battles and lost their lives.

I have to escape, somehow. That'll mean abandoning Princess Silviana, though...

Nazar did not believe this was his time to die.

If he died, no one would take up his noble campaign.

The world was full of people who thought only of themselves. If he died, the losing nations would soon be swallowed up and eradicated, and war against the Alliance of Four would begin anew.

No, even sooner than that, Carrot would revive Geddigs, and the Alliance of Four would all perish.

But just as that thought occurred to him, Nazar's body suddenly felt lighter.

The glow of his equipment strengthened in brilliance for a moment, and then the light disappeared altogether.

But Nazar couldn't move.

The broad back of an orc loomed above him.

"Stand aside."

Nazar immediately shifted a step to the side.

He thought Bash was speaking to him.

But Bash wasn't even facing him, and he ignored him when he moved.

The charm, huh...?

Now suddenly able to move his feet, Nazar understood that the charm cast upon him had been lifted.

Carrot's eyes had stopped glowing red.

"Huh...?"

Carrot looked dumbfounded for a moment but immediately pursed her lips.

"No, I won't stand aside," declared Bash.

"...What?"

"You probably already figured it out, Lord Bash, with your great intellect, but this woman was trying to trick you. She was planning to seduce you, insist that you assaulted her, and besmirch the name of the orcs in front of the other races."

"...Hmm."

"It would appear that the Orc Hero had forced himself upon a beastkin princess. Even if they knew it was all just a lie, the beastkin royal family would surely swallow it simply because they hate orcs. They would jump on any opportunity to wipe out the orcs once and for all," said Carrot.

When Nazar heard that, he thought it sounded entirely plausible.

There was no way to deny it. Princess Silviana's hatred of the orcs was well-known.

After that scene the other day in the royal palace, rumors were circulating that she'd changed her mind. But any who truly knew her knew there was no way she would let go of such intense hatred so quickly.

And if she'd approached Bash, revenge was surely her only motive.

Carrot grabbed Silviana by the hair and lifted her head off the ground.

"I'm right, aren't I?"

Silviana smiled fearlessly through her painful grimace.

"...Th-that's not true! I adore Lord Bash! You just want him for yourself! You're just jealous because Lord Bash and I get along so well!"

Anyone could tell she was lying.

Her eyes were swimming with tears, her voice was tremulous, and she was dripping with cold sweat.

Bash had a slightly confused look on his face, but when the fairy whispered something into his ear, he nodded.

"I see."

Bash's words sounded like a sigh of disappointment.

As if he was realizing it had all been fake, right from the start.

"See? You were too sloppy about it. Of course you'd get found out."

"Y-you're just mad your plan failed! Look, Lord Bash, here's the proof! This wench is trying to paint me as a scapegoat!"

Silviana's denial was incoherent, desperate, and painful to witness.

Eventually, Carrot sighed, as if she couldn't stand to hear any more, and turned to Bash.

"Lord Bash, you know I'm right. A lying princess who tries to trick the great heroes of other countries, a human prince who deceives by pretending to be someone else... See how the races of the former Alliance of Four treat orcs and succubi as lesser beings? See how they mock us?"

Carrot reached out to Bash.

As if seeking a handshake.

"Lord Bash. We intend to fight, to regain the pride of all the races of the Coalition of Seven. Please, take my hand, and let us fight together."

She pleaded with utmost sincerity.

When Bash nodded, Carrot continued, taking his nod for agreement.

"To tell you the truth, we don't have much time. So I will give you a detailed explanation of the strategy later. First, let's kill this lying princess and this conniving prince and escape from this place."

Apparently, Carrot hadn't already recruited Bash. She was attempting to do so now.

No matter what Nazar said, Bash would not change his mind.

Nazar had no power to reach him.

From Bash's point of view, coming along quietly with a human nobody known as Errol... That would only lead to him receiving humiliating treatment at the royal palace. And if it was found out that Errol was really Nazar, Bash would be the target of anger.

It would look like the beastkin and humans had conspired to corner Bash.

It would be too late for apologies or explanations.

Errol should have gone about as Nazar from the beginning and apologized on Bash's behalf when he heard about the disturbance at the royal palace.

Nazar had been looking for the conspirators who sought to revive Geddigs. He hadn't had time to think about Bash.

And Silviana's final lie was the last straw.

She could have apologized. But she lied instead.

And she had looked down on Carrot.

From Bash's point of view, Silviana standing up for him after he was mocked and taunted... That was nothing more than a betrayal in disguise.

"..."

Bash was silent for a few seconds, then glanced at Nazar.

...I guess this is the end.

In that moment, Nazar prepared himself for death.

He'd been planning to flee, but there didn't seem to be any way out of this.

The Orc Hero's aura was overwhelming, as strong as any warrior who ever lived.

Nazar was widely regarded as the strongest human swordsman, but maybe because of that, he was able to identify a stronger foe.

He was prepared to fight. He was prepared to die.

That's all there was to it.

Victory seemed futile. Escape seemed impossible.

He recalled how it had been right after defeating Geddigs. The despair he'd felt when Bash had appeared.

"I can't do that."

But Bash wasn't even looking at Nazar.

"Huh?"

Carrot's dumbfounded voice sounded especially loud.

"Why not?! The other day, you said we would fight together!"

"I owe this man a debt."

"A debt?!"

"Indeed."

"So you're just fine with the way things are?!"

"...What's wrong with the way things are?"

"Succubi are starving! Even the children! Isn't that true of the orcs, too?! In fact, after the war, many orc warriors were dissatisfied with the Orc King's reign and left to go rogue! Many proud warriors... Veteran warriors! Even Gagan lying there was a man who'd reached the rank of battalion commander, but he couldn't even have a woman, so he had no choice but to leave his home! He came to me, begging to be my slave, if only I'd give him a woman in return! He groveled before a succubus like me! And now look at what's become of him!"

Bash looked at Gagan's charred corpse.

Nazar could not read Bash's expression.

He just seemed sort of sad.

"I understand how Gagan felt, but..."

After saying that, Bash was silent for a while. He seemed to be choosing his words carefully.

Finally, Bash continued in a quiet voice...

"...that is the price of defeat."

Hearing that, Carrot looked shocked and cast her gaze down.

"...Ah yes, of course. Bash, being the great man you are, you came to this place with a fierce determination."

After saying that, Carrot slowly stood up.

Her face looked tearful. It was like she was seeing off a warrior who was throwing himself into a battle he could not win.

"No matter what I say, you won't change your mind?"

"No."

"...Even if I tell you that we could resurrect the Demon Lord Geddigs?"

"That changes nothing."

Carrot slowly closed her eyes and exhaled.

"Okay... Even if you walk a different path, you still have my utmost respect as a warrior."

"And you, mine."

At those words, Carrot's cheeks blushed slightly, and her mouth loosened.

However, the smile vanished as quickly as it had appeared.

Her expression stiffened. She went from a woman admiring her hero to a hardened warrior herself.

"I will see my mission through, even if it means taking you out."

"...I understand."

Carrot held up her fists and advanced on Bash.

There was no need for further discussion between the two warriors.

"Former First Battalion General Commander of the Succubi Queendom, Carrot the Breathstealer."

Carrot had been named aloud.

She fluffed up her hair and smiled with her eyes.

"Former Budarth Troop Warrior of the Orc Kingdom, Orc Hero Bash."

Bash was also named aloud.

It was a bold exchange, but there seemed to be some hesitation in her voice. Because Bash was able to sympathize with the current plight of the succubi, Carrot must have been feeling reluctant to fight him.

"..."

Bash glared at Carrot and raised his own fists.

Neither brandished a weapon. Both Bash and Carrot had surrendered their weapons when entering the royal palace.

Only Nazar, who had obtained permission in advance, had a weapon on his person.

But he didn't move. It was a perfect opportunity to escape, but he didn't.

I see... So that's how it is...

He was very impressed.

This is rather splendid...

Nazar was unaware of their relationship.

He did not know what kind of conversation the two had had in private. But Carrot's proposal wasn't really a bad one for Bash. If war broke out, the scrap-loving orc could battle to his heart's content.

The woman would be pleased, too. In fact, she was saying that she'd go the distance.

And if Geddigs was resurrected, victory was certain. Bash would get everything he wanted.

But Bash had said no. Because he was indebted to Nazar.

Indebted... True, Nazar had gotten Bash over the border.

He'd also guided him to the royal palace. But then, when Nazar thought about the trouble that came after that, he felt bad.

Why would Bash be grateful for that? Nazar wouldn't have blamed Bash for thinking Nazar had led him into a trap.

But Bash saw himself as indebted.

Indebted...to Nazar.

For that reason, he rejected Carrot's offer.

Nazar's chest blazed with warmth.

Bash had accepted defeat while preserving what remained of his orcish pride. He believed the orcs, too, should change with the times.

Or perhaps he was taking a stance against the orc species as a whole.

Accept defeat? We have to fight. Fighting, capturing, and defiling women was the supreme way of life for us orcs.

But Bash forsook all that and decided to go with what he thought was right.

Nazar thought Bash's goals were similar to his own. They were going about things differently, but ultimately, they wanted the same thing.

No.

Surely his goal was even nobler than Nazar's.

Surely this Orc Hero was looking further ahead.

Something beyond this peaceful era. Something even Nazar could not yet see.

Otherwise, why would he say he was indebted to Nazar—the one who had hidden his true identity?

Houston, now I understand why you spoke so highly of Lord Bash in your letter.

Nazar could not flee.

Nazar resolved to stay and witness the choice, the battle, the pride of the orc he saw before him.

12

The Hero vs. the Breathstealer

Bash had no idea what was going on.

He'd received the letter and arrived at the Sacred Tree around the time the speeches were about to begin.

He was sure he wasn't late. However, for some reason there were more people besides Silviana present beneath the Sacred Tree.

For some reason, Carrot had her foot on top of Silviana.

For some reason, Gagan was dead after being cleaved neatly in two.

For some reason, Nazar had hidden his true identity and called himself Errol.

The three of them seemed to be in some sort of disagreement, but Bash couldn't possibly guess at the circumstances behind it. It was beyond his capacity to figure out.

(...What's going on?)

(I don't know, Boss, but...from what I've seen, it appears to be some sort of love quarrel.)

Zell seemed to know what was going on right away.

As expected of Bash's ever-reliable comrade.

(A love quarrel?)

(I read about them in books a while back, Boss. It seems humans and beasts fight duels when they both have their eye on the same romantic interest.)

(...Carrot and Silviana had a duel? Then what are Nazar and Gagan doing here?)

(My guess is Carrot has feelings for you, Boss. So she challenged Silviana, who you've been courting, to a duel. Carrot won, obviously. Then Gagan, who has the hots for Carrot, showed up, and Nazar showed up because he has a thing for Silviana. At that point, it became an all-out brawl, and Nazar ended up taking out Gagan. So with *that* settled, it was time for the two victors to duel to the death. But as expected, it looks like the human male was no match for Carrot's charm attack, so this should be over pretty quickly.)

This fairy wasn't known as Detective Zell for nothing. They could paint a detailed picture of what had occurred after only a few seconds on the scene.

There was no case they couldn't crack.

...Though in truth, love quarrels didn't typically play out in tournament fashion.

(I see.)

But Bash was utterly convinced by Zell's *sound* reasoning.

The long-winded explanation was a bit too complicated for him, and to be perfectly honest, he could only understand about half of it. But if two orcs wanted to marry the same woman, then it would be common sense for them to fight to the death and for the victor to take the woman's hand in marriage.

Assuming other races had similar quarrels, this situation made that much more sense to Bash.

(But still, Nazar sure is unlucky, huh? After all, the princess only has eyes for you, Boss.)

(I can't blame him, though. She's incredibly attractive.)

Normally, Bash would be angered by Nazar trying to interfere with the woman he was pursuing himself. But Bash owed Nazar a great debt.

He had provided Bash with the magazine, truly a sacred treasure of the human royal family.

Without that magazine, Bash wouldn't have been able to get this far with Silviana, that much was certain.

Anyway, Silviana was going to have sex with Bash tonight and then become his bride. In light of this, Bash was willing to be mature about things and overlook Nazar's actions.

(What are you going to do, Boss?)

(Help Silviana and repay my debt to Nazar.)

Killing two birds with one stone.

If Bash dispatched Carrot and foiled her plot, he could show Silviana his good side, and it would also lead nicely into him repaying his debt to Nazar.

So Bash made his move.

He moved in front of Nazar, who had been paralyzed by Carrot's charm, and advanced on Carrot.

"Carrot."

"Yes. I've been waiting for you, Lord Bash."

Carrot wore the cultural garb of the succubus, attire that seemed almost designed to arrest Bash's eyes and his life force. Beneath her tight clothing, an unbelievably buxom body was ready to burst free.

If Bash hadn't been a virgin, he would have easily been swayed and let Carrot do whatever she wanted.

But that was not the case.

With an iron will, Bash looked away and turned to Silviana.

"Stand aside."

"Huh...?"

Carrot looked dumbfounded for a moment but immediately scowled.

"No, I won't stand aside."

"...What?"

"You probably already figured it out, Lord Bash, with your great intellect, but this woman was trying to trick you. She was planning to seduce you, insist that you assaulted her, and besmirch the name of the orcs in front of the other races."

"...Hmm."

"It would appear that the Orc Hero had forced himself upon a beastkin princess. Even if they knew it was all just a lie, the beastkin royal family would surely swallow it simply because they hate orcs. They would jump on any opportunity to wipe out the orcs once and for all."

Carrot grabbed Silviana by the hair and lifted her head off the ground.

"I'm right, aren't I?"

Silviana smiled fearlessly through her painful grimace.

"...Th-that's not true! I adore Lord Bash! You just want him for yourself! You're just jealous because Lord Bash and I get along so well!"

Then Zell whispered into Bash's ear once more.

(Aha! It looks like our deduction was correct.)

(I see.)

The power of the press was a scary thing.

With the magazine's help, Bash had somehow managed to charm not only Silviana but Carrot, too.

It was the same as during the war.

If one wielded magic weapons and talismans they had no experience with, they could end up cutting their allies without even realizing it.

"See? You were too sloppy about it. Of course you'd get found out."

"Y-you're just mad your plan failed! Look, Lord Bash, here's the proof! This wench is trying to paint me as a scapegoat!

"Lord Bash, you know I'm right. A lying princess who tries to trick the great heroes of other countries, a human prince who deceives by pretending to be someone else... See how the races of the former Alliance of Four treat orcs and succubi as lesser beings? See how they mock us?"

Mock them... True, Silviana's behavior didn't communicate any sort of advantage.

It was not the demeanor of a loser. It was the desperate act of someone who knew victory was futile and yet fought to the death anyway. And Nazar had disguised himself as Errol. From the point of view of someone who'd been caught by these traps, it did seem rather like mockery.

"Lord Bash. We intend to fight, to regain the pride of all the races of the Coalition of Seven. Please, take my hand, and let us fight together."

Carrot reached out to Bash.

Her plump breasts jiggled, which was very eye-catching.

It could even be a succubus-style proposal.

The other day, when Bash had said he'd like to fight with her again... Was this how she'd misinterpreted those words?

"To tell you the truth, we don't have much time. So I will give you a detailed explanation of the strategy later. First, let's kill this lying princess and this conniving prince and escape from this place."

But Bash had already made up his mind. He felt regret over having misled her, but he wanted to be with Silviana. And he owed Nazar a great debt.

He couldn't kill either of them.

"I can't do that."

"Huh?"

Carrot's shocked expression ate at Bash.

He must have made that same sort of face when he had been rejected, time after time.

"Why not?! The other day, you said we would fight together!"

"I owe this man a debt."

"A debt?!"

"Indeed."

"So you're just fine with the way things are?!"

"...What's wrong with the way things are?"

Bash's question was sincere.

"Succubi are starving! Even the children! Isn't that true of the orcs, too?! In fact, after the war, many orc warriors were dissatisfied with the Orc King's reign and left to go rogue! Many proud warriors... Veteran warriors! Even Gagan lying there was a man who'd reached the rank of battalion commander, but he couldn't even have a woman, so he had no choice but to leave his home! He came to me, begging to be my slave, if only I'd give him a woman in return! He groveled before a succubus like me! And now look at what's become of him!"

Bash tilted his head slightly, surprised by the sudden change in topic.

Indeed, the orcs were probably worse off than they had been in the past, during the war.

Were a few children going hungry? Probably. But that was the way things were. It had been that way since the days of the war.

It was true, too, that there had been an exodus of rogue orcs, dissatisfied with the way things were in the orc country. Unable to go along with the Orc King's decisions and accept defeat, they instead chose to leave.

"I understand how Gagan felt, but..."

Yes. Bash understood how Gagan felt.

Gagan became a stray orc early on and quickly left the orc country.

Bash hadn't been privy to his reasoning, but generally, when orcs absconded, it was because they were seeking either a fight or a woman.

If Bash hadn't been a virgin. If he hadn't been an Orc Hero... If Carrot hadn't been a succubus... If it wasn't a known fact that Bash attempting to lose his virgin status with a succubus would lead straight to a future of wizardry...then maybe he would have agreed to become Carrot's slave.

Gagan had come seeking a fight in order to make Carrot his. And he had lost and died.

His actions went against the word of the Orc King, but they were undeniably orcish acts. And his end, too, was in a sense very orclike.

"That is the price of defeat."

"...Ah yes, of course. Bash, being the great man you are, you came to this place with a fierce determination."

Determination. Yes, Bash came determined to mate with Silviana.

A princess was the perfect choice for a Hero's wife. Bash would finally be able to return home with his head held high.

By the time they reached the orc country, Silviana would be pregnant. Since she was a beastkin, she would probably give birth to five or six pups.

And by then, Bash would be able to have sex without feeling awkward or self-conscious.

"No matter what I say, you won't change your mind?"

"No."

"...Even if I tell you that we could resurrect the Demon Lord Geddigs?"

"That changes nothing."

A strange exchange, but even if Geddigs was resurrected that very night, Bash's resolve would not waver.

He would overcome the obstacle in his path and rescue Silviana.

"Okay... Even if you walk a different path, you still have my utmost respect as a warrior."

"And you, mine."

"I will see my mission through, even if it means taking you out."

"...I understand."

Bash could understand the sequence of events well.

Orcs fought to obtain the sexual partner they desired.

If Carrot wanted to have Bash and was now challenging him to a fight, then Bash would win the battle and see Carrot off.

"Former First Battalion General Commander of the Succubi Queendom, Carrot the Breathstealer."

"Former Budarth Troop Warrior of the Orc Kingdom, Orc Hero Bash."

Bash spoke grandly.

Then he roared.

"Graaagh!!!"

His war cry marked the official commencement of battle.

■

A one-on-one battle between an orc and a succubus.

Nazar honestly thought Bash had no chance of victory.

No matter how strong he was, how famous he was for his physical prowess even among other races, he was still a male. Moreover, Carrot's charm was so strong that even a man with high magic resistance like Nazar had ended up falling victim to her alluring magic.

Carrot would have Bash charmed in seconds, and then all she would have to do was mount him and proceed to drain his energy.

Nazar was willing to help Bash if it came to that.

He'd made up his mind to watch until the end, but he couldn't just let the orc die.

But that didn't happen.

What's going on…?

Bash leaped into the fight without hesitation.

Unbelievable! He completely nullified the charm somehow!

But it didn't appear as though Bash had done anything at all.

It didn't even look like he was wearing any special equipment.

However, it would be impossible for any man to move so swiftly against a succubus without dispelling her charm magic.

…He might actually be able to win…

In the space of a gulp from Nazar, Bash had closed in on Carrot and was now swinging a punch at that bewitching face of hers.

Such violence... A hit like that one could shatter boulders.

"Hmph!"

Carrot blocked and parried the blow with the side of her fist.

Without being knocked back at all, Carrot dealt Bash a full-body blow.

Carrot's thin, small, but tightly clenched fist pierced Bash's side.

An onlooker would have seen how sharp that hook-thrust really was.

The succubus's martial arts move, the hook-thrust, penetrated the skin and muscles, crushed the bones, pierced the internal organs, and invited death with a single blow.

And this blow had been dealt by the Breathstealer herself, the most skilled succubus warrior of all. Even a half-hearted punch from her could knock someone's upper body clean off their legs. Her ability to magically augment her physical strength was just that great.

"Graaarrr!!!"

But Bash was unmoved.

Though her blow was indeed strengthened by magical means, the damage she dealt to Bash seemed rather minimal.

"Hyah!"

It was unclear whether Carrot had realized this, as she drove her fist once again into Bash's body.

A forward fist, a back fist, a roundhouse kick, an elbow strike, a knee kick, a water-surface kick, a sobat, a heel drop...

She hit Bash with move after move, without any hesitation at all.

But they were everyday attacks. These weren't the moves that made succubus martial arts so feared.

Carrot jumped. Flapping her wings, she sprayed the surroundings with dust.

A double sobat, a wing strike, a reverse heel drop...

It was a continuous attack—the kind of attack humans and beastkin weren't capable of. And it was certainly beyond the skill level of orcs and ogres. With this move, she could easily target parts that were normally considered difficult to hit. If a human martial artist saw such a display, he would let out a cry of admiration and wonder why he, too, was not born a succubus.

"...!"

It was a truly artistic display of martial arts, but the only thing that actually did any real damage was that first hook thrust.

Bash's guard was solid, preventing all blows to vital points, and he was quick with a counterattack each time.

His counterattacks, while casual in execution, were as accurate and precise as a dive-bombing fly. If any of these hits landed head-on, they would no doubt break bones, leaving his opponent, Carrot, incapacitated.

She had no choice but to parry them, but even that required delicacy, like a complicated bomb-defusing operation.

Bash overwhelmed Carrot, both offensively and defensively.

He had Carrot on the ropes in no time.

"Guh!"

Before long, Bash's fist penetrated Carrot's defense, sank deeply into her solar plexus, and Carrot was flung across the clearing, to the entrance.

"Gack, guhhh!"

A torrent of blood from Carrot's mouth splattered the surroundings.

Carrot stumbled, buckling at her knees.

She'd meant to guard. She'd cast a magical barrier.

But even with that, her bones were cracked, and her stomach had collapsed.

"...Hee-hee-hee."

Nazar rubbed his chin. How many years had it been since he'd last seen her coughing up blood?

Nazar hadn't seen her in this state since her battle against Liscia.

"So you're really not pulling your punches, are you?"

"Of course not."

At Bash's response, Carrot dragged herself to her feet.

Nazar saw this and felt envious. She must have been feeling so pure right now... So refreshed. After all, the Orc Hero wasn't just playing. He was fighting seriously. As a warrior, there was no greater honor.

"Even so, I'm really...sorry...it looks like we're out of time."

When Carrot muttered those words...

"...!"

...it happened in the blink of an eye.

Yes, a mere flutter of the eyelid. Before anyone even knew what had happened, a woman appeared by the succubus's side.

"..."

A tall, pale-skinned woman wearing a jet black robe so dark it would suffocate even the darkness of a moonless night. Her head bore a goat's skull as an ornament. She looked around and shook her head at Bash's fists and at Carrot on her knees, surrounded by blood and puke.

"Hmm? Lord Bash is siding with the enemy?"

"Yes. I couldn't manage to persuade him."

"I see. What a pity... If even your seduction techniques didn't work, then there is nothing to be done."

"How rude. I, Carrot, am a proud succubus. I don't use my sex appeal against opponents I respect."

"I see."

The woman had two horns on her head and dark circles under her eyes.

In her hand, she held a sticky staff, the tip of which was dripping with something dark, like sludge.

All present knew her by sight.

Nazar spoke the name.

The name of the mage who'd cast all her enemies into eternal darkness, the mage who had been a close aide to Geddigs the Demon Lord.

"Popratika...the Shadow Vortex."

She was a demon mage.

"So did you get it?"

She didn't even look at Nazar and Bash as she spoke to Carrot.

"Yes. Though I was interrupted."

"...I'm surprised you're still alive. I can't believe you would fight Lord Bash without your charm."

"Well, I'm still standing, aren't I?"

"Barely." Popratika lowered her gaze to the ground with a half smile. "Nevertheless, it's a shame."

All of a sudden, the shadows on the ground expanded.

It was like something had come rising up from the ground itself—an undulating shadow that covered the both of them.

"But we still have a chance."

"We do."

And then, with a *bang*, darkness swallowed the two of them.

"Wait!"

Nazar screamed and dashed forward, but it was too late.

When the darkness faded, there was nothing there.

It happened so quickly.

But perhaps this was to have been expected. Carrot had said something about running out of time, but still, she'd shown no sign of fleeing the area on foot.

And with Thunder Sonia, her mortal enemy, present in the palace, she wouldn't have gotten far like that anyway.

From the beginning, she'd probably been banking on being able to use Popratika's Shadowstep to escape.

"There's no way we can pursue them like this."

Nazar came to a stop, muttering to himself.

The Shadowstep was a secret form of demon magic.

It enabled a caster to move from shadow to shadow in an instant. It couldn't be used to transport a large number of people at once, and there were various restrictions on where one could travel. But there was no better method for sending small numbers of important individuals from one place to another.

Only a handful of demon mages could use it. It belonged to the highest level of magical spells.

Originally, the distance that could be traveled was short, but Popratika's Shadowstep was something else entirely.

There was one particular incident that was widely spoken of. The ogre known as the Berserk Gardener, having been captured and locked up in the beastkin fortress, managed to escape beyond the palace walls this way.

It would make sense that Carrot had escaped somewhere far beyond reach.

In that case, pursuit was futile. All that remained was to make a report to the individuals who would no doubt soon arrive, attracted by the commotion.

Depending on how that went, Bash could be in for some undue suspicion.

Nazar rubbed his chin and lowered his tense shoulders.

"Lord Bash. First, I will explain this entire situation, and..."

Nazar turned, looking behind him as he spoke. Then he stopped and stared.

The orc man and beastkin woman were frozen there, gazing intensely at each other.

13

The Proposal

Silviana was nervous.

Carrot, who was a threat, had withdrawn. But Silviana's plans had been completely exposed.

Could she be relieved? Or should she keep her guard raised?

Now Bash was standing directly in front of her, staring.

She had no idea what he was thinking.

As a tactician, a war strategist, and as someone belonging to the royal court, she'd always thought of herself as someone who was good at reading the intentions of others. But she'd never had to scrutinize an orc's facial expressions before.

"..."

Her mind was completely blank.

Usually, she was quick on the draw. But in this moment, she had nothing to offer.

There was too much going on, and she had no idea how to proceed.

At the very least, she needed to tell the Queen and her sisters that, due to her own blunder, the seed of the Sacred Tree had been stolen.

But before that, she first needed to escape the threat she was being directly faced with.

She couldn't afford to be ripped limb from limb by an enraged orc...

"Oh! Lord Bash, I was so scared...!"

...Therefore, Silviana committed to the lie.

She flung herself into Bash's chest, playing the part of a princess who'd been held captive.

Her performance now was even better than when she was being stepped on by

Carrot. She wondered if things would have gone differently, if only she'd played the part of the damsel in distress earlier.

Even though she knew, already, that it was too late.

If the orc was the type to fall for her tricks this easily, then he would have ravaged her already, sparking a new war between beastkin and orcs.

"Silviana."

Bash got down on one knee and gazed up at her.

He clutched a single white flower in his fist.

A white flower. It was the custom among beastkin for a suitor to present a white flower when asking a lady for her hand in marriage.

"Please marry me, be my wife, and start a family with me."

His words were so sincere. And so plainly spoken.

If only Bash weren't an orc, Silviana thought she might have been swept off her feet. She might have started nodding before she'd even processed it.

"Oh... Um..."

Right. Nodding was the move here, wasn't it?

She had summoned Bash here, expecting this, hadn't she?

She would nod, let Bash take her on the spot, and then claim it wasn't consensual. That was her plan... But she couldn't go through with it...

...because there was someone present.

Nazar, the Human Prince.

"Hmm... I see. Heh, well, how about if I serve as witness?" Nazar said with a chuckle.

If he was a witness to it, then Silviana wouldn't be able to get away with the lie.

Nazar was a human prince and a hero. His word was especially respected among humans. As long as he was present, then no matter how big a fuss Silviana kicked up, he would be able to expose her lie in seconds.

Or...perhaps she could claim that both Bash *and* Nazar had assaulted her.

If she did that, and those lies were swallowed...then she would probably invite war with the humans as well...

The elves would probably ally with the beastkin, what with the recent wedding joining their two races and all. But they wouldn't want to directly do battle against the humans.

On the other hand, the humans and orcs, angered by the besmirching of their lauded heroes, would crush the beastkin with a fiery indignity.

The beastkin would die out, eventually fading away as a race.

Or they might even end up being a vassal state of the orcs.

She couldn't let that happen.

"I... I... I think..."

"Now listen, I'm sure Lord Bash will be gracious, no matter what your answer may be. But if you don't take this man seriously, you'll have *me* to answer to. As a war buddy of the great Hero Leto, who was felled by this great orc...as a man who himself was saved from certain death by this orc...I swear that if you make a fool of this most proud warrior, I will see that you suffer."

"...M-make a fool of him?"

Silviana gnashed her teeth.

"Princess Silviana, it appears you've always said you held a grudge against the orc who besmirched Leto's honor, but do you really think that's what this man has done?"

"..."

"Were you paying attention to that display just now? *Were* you? If so, then how can you continue to think this man is without honor?"

All right, all right. She knew the truth of it...

It was as Bash said the other day.

He hadn't left Leto's corpse to rot for the fun of it. The truth was that Bash was proud to have fought the Beastkin Hero and barely claimed victory. It was a war tale worth boasting about. And Bash himself had even said that he regretted leaving the Beastkin Hero's body where it lay.

And Silviana even understood why Bash had done so as well.

If she had been present, as a tactician for the Coalition of Seven, and if Bash had asked her for instruction...well, she would have given Bash the exact same orders.

And that wasn't all.

Bash's behavior had been exemplary ever since he'd set foot into beastkin country.

She'd blocked her ears and eyes to him, dismissed him as just another orc, but when she thought about it rationally...Bash's behavior was worthy of respect.

He'd worn the right clothes, read books on etiquette, held back his base urges, and made a concerted effort to entertain and woo Silviana.

If he'd been a human or an elf, his actions wouldn't have warranted that much credit, sure. But Lord Bash was an orc. This sort of behavior didn't come naturally to orcs. Silviana could agree with that, easily.

In all likelihood, no other orc would have acted the way Bash had.

Just like Carrot said, Bash had studied. He'd probably felt as though he had to go to those lengths to be accepted, since he was an orc.

But in truth, the princesses (Silviana included) hadn't accepted him.

Thinking about it now... It was narrow-minded. But no one had expected an orc to go to such lengths. They hadn't thought to give orcs that much credit at all.

Not only was Bash ejected from the venue, but he faced constant taunts after that from all the princesses.

That must have been humiliating.

In the midst of such humiliation, the prospect of teaming up with Carrot to revive Geddigs must have been tempting.

With the situation being what it was, both Silviana and Nazar had fully expected Bash to cross over to the dark side.

But Bash had rejected Carrot's proposal. He'd chosen his own path.

He was really...genuinely...a good man.

All the big names in the Coalition of Seven were highly respected warriors.

When you really think about it, what I'm actually doing is taking the good name of the beastkin... Of Uncle Leto... And...

Thinking that far, Silviana felt her strength drain from her body.

"...Lord Bash."

"Hmm?"

Bash looked...happy.

Was he thinking that he was finally about to get revenge on the one who'd tricked him?

No, he wasn't that coldhearted. Perhaps he was only teasing?

Silviana couldn't read that expression all that well, but it seemed that way to her.

"I'm sorry I deceived you."

"...What?"

"The truth is, Carrot was right about everything... I was planning on entrapping you and possibly even destroying the whole orc race."

"...Mm."

"My reason was revenge... I thought my uncle, the Hero Leto, had been dishonored... But I was mistaken. I heard what you said, but I was caught up in my emotions, allowed Carrot's sweet words to poison my ear, and almost made an irreparable mistake."

Silviana knelt.

Crossing her arms before her, she placed her arms against the ground, placed her forehead on her arms, and capitulated.

Like a wild beast admitting defeat.

Before, she would have died before saying what she was about to say next to an orc.

"Please, forgive me."

The words rolled off her tongue with ease.

"..."

Bash looked to his companion, the fairy.

He certainly hadn't expected Silviana to apologize so easily.

The fairy whispered something in Bash's ear.

Bash nodded slightly and spoke to Silviana again.

"Mm... So does this mean you won't be my wife?"

No doubt this taunt was a cruel suggestion from the fairy.

It seemed as though Bash still meant to humiliate Silviana. Or perhaps Bash actually was being earnest. But the man who'd been silently watching this unfold wasn't about to let it all slide.

"A liar is not worthy to be a companion for a Hero. I must ask you to withdraw your overtly generous offer, Lord Bash."

"...I see. I understand."

Bash slowly stood up and looked up at the sky.

He looked almost deeply sorry that he could not make Silviana his wife.

But why should *he* look sorry?

Confused, Silviana raised her face to look up at Bash...and realized something.

"...?"

Dry leaves were fluttering down from the sky.

It was as if autumn had come. Even though the Red Forest was meant to be full of vibrant leaves all year round.

"What...?!"

Silviana got to her feet and whipped her head around.

Nazar looked in the same direction.

"...No..."

The three of them gazed up at the Sacred Tree.

A huge tree with lush red leaves.

Or at least, that's what it usually looked like.

Now the overgrown leaves were crisp and dry and beginning to fall.

The branches were thinning and slowly beginning to break off with a series of crackling sounds.

The trunk, which was once so full of life, was stripped of its bark and now cracked vertically, as if it had gotten root rot.

"This... This can't be...!"

Throughout history, the Sacred Tree had given the beastkin so much hope. It was a symbol of the enduring spirit of their people...

But now, the Sacred Tree was withering.

EPİLOGUE

Two full days had passed since the Sacred Tree withered.

The sudden change in the Sacred Tree caused an uproar at the wedding venue.

The wedding was halted, and the soldiers who'd come to check on the situation of the Sacred Tree immediately rushed Bash, thinking he was responsible. Until the Human Prince Nazar gave an explanation, that is.

He explained that certain individuals were actively plotting for the resurrection of Geddigs, that they had stolen the seed of the Sacred Tree, and that as a result, the Sacred Tree had withered... And that both Nazar and Silviana, on the verge of being murdered by those salacious individuals, had been saved by the Orc Hero Bash.

Nazar avoided naming Carrot and Popratika, so at first the soldiers treated his story with suspicion. But then Silviana admitted that the situation had been facilitated by her own lack of foresight, and the soldiers immediately headed off to report all of this to their superiors.

The two accompanied them to help explain, and for the time being, Bash was allowed to go free.

Upon receiving the report, those in charge of the beastkin country's affairs took the situation very seriously indeed.

The resurrection of the Demon Lord Geddigs.

The return of that damnable war.

It was something that had to be prevented by all those wishing for peace in the present day. Intel would be shared to every foreign country with haste, a subjugation force would be organized, and action would be taken immediately to prevent the resurrection of Geddigs.

And most importantly, a public gag order was placed on the info that individuals were out there trying to revive Geddigs.

It would be bad enough if the news spread among the races of the Alliance of Four: the humans, the elves, the dwarves, and the beastkin. But if the news got out to the Coalition of Seven, there was the possibility of a large-scale uprising.

Those countries may even have proceeded to breach the peace treaty.

Not all of them were the upstanding individuals Bash was.

Bash had returned to the inn and was making preparations to continue his trip while the beastkin country began to quietly panic.

He had been so close...

He'd done everything by the book. The atmosphere had been perfect each time as well. He'd even caught the attention of a woman he wasn't even pursuing! Nothing should have gone wrong.

There was one thing, though. The words, written on the last page of the magazine... They had become reality.

Yes, the last page of the magazine.

It read:

If your date is looking for money, or if she wants to trick you in some way, then ultimately, marriage may be impossible. Consider yourself played!

Silviana herself had clearly stated that she had been playing Bash all along, and that her intention had been to deceive him, so there was no point bothering with her any further.

To be honest, Bash was feeling rather deflated.

But the magazine's teachings had not been wrong.

As proof, Carrot had fallen in love with Bash overnight. Silviana might have been a lost cause, but Bash had a hunch that the next woman he met would be the one.

A few days later, Bash went back to the bar where he'd met Carrot.

However, with the Sacred Tree withering and the wedding ceremony being canceled, the cheerful atmosphere in the town had completely disappeared, and there were almost no women, let alone men, in the bar. During the day, the town was in a frenzy, and men and women alike had begun to shoot Bash dirty looks, as if the war had been reignited already.

Yes, Bash was certain he'd manage to find a woman with his next attempt, but then again, the magazine did say that a jovial public mood was the best setting for wooing a woman.

In other words, in this distinctly *un*jovial atmosphere, his chances were slim.

Even Bash had to conclude that it would be difficult to find a bride in this town, and so he made preparations to hit the road again.

"...But where to next?"

He wasn't sure.

"It's a tough call, ain't it, Boss? From here, it might not be a bad idea to head to the human enclave."

"It's pretty far away..."

No more dwarves. Because of the Thunder Sonia incident, the elves were out, too.

That left only the humans.

But the human country was much too far from beastkin country.

"Oh, are you leaving?"

Someone was addressing the two as they hashed out their plans.

"Nazar, huh?"

At the entrance of the inn stood a man. A man wearing a mask and strumming an instrument. A terrible sound emanated from it today as well.

"I'm sorry, but could you call me Errol while I'm wearing this mask?"

"I see. Thank you for your help this far, Errol."

Errol had certainly been of great assistance to Bash.

But even with Errol's help, Bash had struck out yet again. He could only conclude that this time, luck had not been on his side.

On the battlefield, you can do everything perfectly and still lose.

That's just how it was.

"Where are you going next?"

"...I haven't decided yet."

"You mean to say you can't stay a while longer?"

"I can't. I don't have much time left."

Many days had passed since Bash had departed the orc land.

Technically, he still had a reasonable amount of time, but he didn't want to waste a second. His thirtieth birthday was drawing ever closer.

"I see... If you haven't decided where to go, mind if I give you a suggestion?"

"Certainly. I trust your opinion."

"It's an honor to hear you say that... For now, I'd like to advise you to go to the demon country."

"...Demon country...?"

Those words reminded Bash of the demon mage he had glimpsed only the other day.

Popratika the Shadow Vortex. Bash had gotten the impression that she was somewhat dark and melancholy, but she was undeniably beautiful.

Come to think of it, most of the demon women Bash had seen so far had been very attractive.

"...Demons would accept an orc?"

The reason orcs didn't usually consider demon women when hunting for a mate was that they always rejected orcs.

During the war, demons were overwhelmingly superior.

Demon women wouldn't give orcs the time of day, and so the orcs had given up on them, dismissing them as out of reach.

Even privately fantasizing about a demon woman was said to be offensive to them.

"Oh, you'll be fine."

"...You think so?"

"Yeah. Actually, I think you're the only one who can do it. You're the only one who can persuade them that the war is truly over."

"I see..."

The war was over.

Both orcs and demons alike had lost the war, and the unbalanced relationship between the two races already dissolved.

In this era of peace, one could woo a mate instead of taking them by force. One could marry for love...so it should be possible even for Bash, an orc, to get with a demon woman. Of course, even so, it would be extremely difficult. After all, traditionally, demon women thought themselves to be too good for orcs.

"Even a demon would have to hear out an Orc Hero."

There. Nazar had just reassured Bash that success was indeed possible.

"...I understand. If that's what you suggest, then I will give it a try."

Bash nodded vigorously.

After all, to Bash, the words of Errol, the emissary of love and peace, were akin to a gospel truth.

"I thought you might say that."

Nazar withdrew a letter from his pocket.

"Once you get to the demon country, give this to the Dark General, Sequence."

"The Dark General... You would even send me with a letter of recommendation?!"

Bash was nodding his head vigorously at the prospect.

The Dark General, Sequence.

A close aide to the Demon Lord Geddigs, he was an exalted figure who'd been in command of the demon army for a long time now.

He was the one holding the demon country together now.

And Sequence had three daughters. All of them were beautiful, and coincidentally, Popratika the Shadow Vortex was one of them.

A letter of recommendation...to Popratika's father.

Even the slow-witted Bash had no trouble understanding exactly what this meant.

The contents of the letter would be Bash's in to wooing Popratika.

"Please understand that I'm not dissing you here, but humans do tend to be better at diplomacy than orcs."

"I appreciate it."

"You're very welcome."

Once he'd grasped the situation, Bash's decision was swift.

"Well then, we shall depart."

"Right. Take care along the way."

Bash got to his feet and exited the inn.

The fairy followed him. As he watched them go, Nazar called out.

"Oh, and, Lord Bash..."

"Hmm?"

"…Thank you."

Bash nodded, looking slightly confused as to why he was being thanked again.

Seeing that, Nazar smiled proudly under his mask.

◼

Silviana was in prison when Bash left.

Although it was known from Nazar's testimony that she had been manipulated by her enemies, she herself had personally asked the Queen for a punishment.

She didn't think that merely going to jail would be sufficient atonement for what she'd done.

She thought that joining the insurrection subjugation team as soon as possible and owning her own part in things was the only way to make amends.

But even so, she needed time to reflect on herself and taste the bitterness of a well-earned punishment.

"…"

Inside the dark, damp prison, Silviana crossed her legs and tried to meditate.

Her heart was filled with regret and thoughts of the future.

She thought hard about what the enemy's next move might be. About how the seed of the Sacred Tree would be used. She came up with various scenarios and countermeasures for them all.

Then one day, a woman came to visit her.

"Silviana."

Hearing the woman's voice, Silviana raised her head.

And when she saw her face, she opened her eyes wide.

Among the sisters, this girl's face was particularly bestial. In fact, she had the head of a dog. But she had a very kind aura.

"Oh! Sister!"

It was Innuella, the third-born princess.

The bride of the wedding that had been canceled due to the current turmoil.

Silviana uncrossed her legs and prostrated herself like a dog.

"I'm so sorry for ruining your celebration with my selfish behavior."

"Yes, it was rather disappointing."

Cold sweat ran down Silviana's forehead at those words.

Her sister had been looking forward to the wedding for a long time. No apology would be enough.

"But that's fine. A wedding is, after all, more of a public event."

"But..."

"It's okay. I'm just happy to be with the man I love."

Innuella smiled cheerfully.

"Anyway, never mind that. You know, since I last saw you, you seem more at peace."

"Do I?"

"Yes. You always seemed so tense whenever we all spoke."

Silviana touched her face.

She hadn't realized it herself, of course, but it made sense to her.

"...The thought of avenging Uncle Leto's murder had always been at the forefront of my mind. I was going to restore the trampled pride of the beastkin, I was going to make the orcs pay..."

"You loved Uncle Leto more than anyone."

"However, when I actually met and spoke with Lord Bash, the Orc Hero, I learned that I had been mistaken. It wasn't true that Bash had made light of his victory over Uncle Leto. It wasn't true that he'd abandoned his corpse as a show of disrespect."

"...It was war."

"Yes. And the war is over. Lord Bash seems to understand that better than anyone. I was stubborn, and I couldn't see the truth. I've been thinking a lot about that."

Bash had shown her the truth.

As she explained to her sister, that fact hit her all over again.

Yes. It was almost as if Lord Bash had been sent to guide her.

A normal man, finding himself accused by Silviana, might try to justify himself.

Instead, Bash calmly told her how he was proud to have fought Uncle Leto.

He had explained with patience, and kindness, as if speaking to a stubborn child.

He was just like...Uncle Leto, who had patiently taught Silviana so much, back when she was just a child. A stubborn child, who'd acted before she thought.

"I only caught a glimpse of Lord Bash at the wedding venue, but his aura reminded me of Uncle Leto."

"Yes."

"Hee-hee, and it seems you agree. I wonder if the next wedding will be a celebration of friendship between orcs and beastkin."

"Please, don't tease me."

Silviana was reminded of Bash's proposal.

She'd told herself it was his way of disarming her, but when she looked back on it, it had been a very passionate proposal. Involuntarily, she flushed.

"The Orc Hero Bash is a great man. Someone like me isn't fit to be his wife."

"Oh, really?"

"Yes, really."

Silviana turned her head away, as if to indicate she was done with that topic.

She didn't want to be seen blushing, on top of her disgrace.

"Anyway, I'm glad you're doing well. I was a bit worried."

"I apologize for worrying you."

But as she spoke, Silviana was thinking.

If only she could become a little less shallow, a little bit more of a well-balanced person... If only she could do that, then perhaps...?

Side Story
The Great Elf Mage Also Departs

A few days after Bash's departure, Thunder Sonia was busy with various tasks.

The beastkin country was in turmoil, and the wedding had been canceled, causing ripples to spread to the elves. Thunder Sonia had been run ragged with diplomatic proceedings.

Although she had acted not as Thunder Sonia but as the Masked Saint, Aurantiaca. As a result, she'd had to do a lot of physical legwork.

But whether she was Thunder Sonia or Aurantiaca, she knew there were forces out there conspiring to resurrect the Demon Lord Geddigs. There was no time for goofing off.

With her many years of experience, Thunder Sonia knew there were things only she could do.

She had to tackle each task one by one and not split her focus.

What those tasks were, however, no one was quite sure.

Today, as well, she found her time being wasted by miscellaneous affairs.

"Haaah, damn it all... What's the point in having all these meetings anyway...?"

Late at night, Thunder Sonia heaved a huge sigh in her room.

Night after night, she was called upon to attend various meetings about what to do next, and she was growing tired of it.

It would've been nice if the meetings were actually constructive. But they never made any progress. All anyone ever seemed to want to talk about was where to place the blame.

But what else could be done? At present, there simply wasn't enough information available.

Plus, gathering information was labor-intensive and time-consuming.

It was clear that Thunder Sonia wouldn't be able to get much information by running around like a headless chicken.

Besides, Thunder Sonia was great at taking action. Once she'd gotten the necessary information, that is...

After grasping the enemy's position and purpose, she would crush them like ants.

The versatility and coping power that came with the elf's great magic skills set her apart from other heroes.

Therefore, as Thunder Sonia, she would've *loooved* to get some info so she could act already!

There was no guarantee she'd even get the information she really needed in this hectic situation. There was also a risk that the members of the Alliance of Four might only get in one another's way.

Excepting the beastkin, whose Sacred Tree had withered right in front of them, the resurrection of Geddigs might sound like nothing more than a nasty hoax to the other races. Elves knew a lot about trees, so if some high-ranking human official suggested that maybe the elves were involved, the dumb dwarves might just start believing it.

Three years had passed since the end of the war. While hatred and resentment born during the war remained, it was also true that there were more people than ever who were completely complacent about peace.

"..."

Bougainvillea, who sat beside Thunder Sonia, silently offered her a glass of water.

Thunder Sonia gulped it down, then looked out the window with her arms crossed.

The view of the beastkin country from this window had not changed at all from a few days ago.

But there was something gloomy about the atmosphere now.

It made sense. The beastkin's beloved Sacred Tree had withered.

Suffocated by the heavy atmosphere, Thunder Sonia thought hard.

"...What should I be doing right now?"

Whatever it was, mopping up the remnants of a ruined wedding certainly wasn't it.

She could immediately return to the elf home country, or to the Shiwanashi Forest, and take command of the response team.

Yes, thinking about it rationally, that was the best course of action.

Most of the elves would spring into action at one command from Thunder Sonia. Having the intelligence department gather information, then considering how best to act depending on what they'd learned...that was always the way things were handled during the war.

But Thunder Sonia was, for once, far away from her country. She was in a position to move freely, without constraint. It would be a shame not to make the most of it.

Also, if she went home, she'd never find herself a husband.

No, Thunder Sonia hadn't given up on her marriage quest just yet.

It's not like it was the highest priority she had, but she certainly didn't want to give up her chances altogether.

Whether the war was going to be resumed or whether it could be stopped, either way, she couldn't deny that she wanted to find herself a husband before that happened.

Thunder Sonia was troubled.

"Bougainvillea...what do you think?"

"I think you should do whatever you want."

The assassin's response to Thunder Sonia was dry. Very dry, indeed.

"The great Thunder Sonia would never act in a manner that would be disadvantageous to the elves. The elders all know that very well."

"Fool. You overestimate them. And as for me, here I am, thinking only of myself... Besides, those fossils are too ancient and stubborn to understand. All they ever have to offer is more complaints!"

In truth, the Elf Senate wouldn't make a peep no matter what Thunder Sonia did, as long as it was for the good of the elves.

Yes... As long as it was for the good of the elves...

If it was revealed that Thunder Sonia was still hoping to get married, the Senate would be enraged. And not only them. Aconitum would roll his eyes, too.

Romance? At your *age?* they would all say.

"Hee-hee. But everything you do is for the good of the elves, Thunder Sonia."

It was possible that even Bougainvillea would be irritated if she knew the truth. Yes, she'd be annoyed for sure. *You say all this when your true intent is to chase after some pathetic man?...*she would say.

So Thunder Sonia could not speak her true conundrum aloud.

She would have to decide for herself.

"It is impossible to separate Thunder Sonia from the elf race she has always served. Everyone thinks so. So act as you see fit, and whatever choice you make will be the right one."

"...As I see fit? Seriously? What if I take your advice and go off hunting for men? What would you do then? A different man every night. Unscrupulous men, even!"

"Ha-ha-ha! If you were capable of doing that, you'd already have at least one or two grandchildren..."

"..."

Touché, Thunder Sonia thought.

"It's okay. Everyone knows you. No matter what Thunder Sonia says or does, she would never, ever turn her back on her people."

"No, of course I wouldn't. It wouldn't be a laughing matter if my country was destroyed while I was off hunting for love."

Thunder Sonia glared out the window, annoyed by the fruitlessness of this conversation.

Then she spotted a suspicious-looking man out there.

It looked like he was sneaking out of the grounds.

"...That man..."

Thunder Sonia, recognizing the man's attire, rose from her chair.

"Hey, where are you going?"

Thunder Sonia's booming voice stopped the man just as he was about to disappear into the darkness.

"What's this? Masked Saint, Aurantiaca. A woman of your advanced age wandering around late at night like this will be suspected of being an assassin, you know."

"Let people think what they want. There's nothing shady about what *I'm* up to.

But what about you? Why are you trying to sneak away in the dark like this? What have you done? I won't tell, so you may as well spit it out, Lord Nazar."

Bougainvillea, listening to this exchange, thought to herself, *Wow, sometimes she really does talk like an old granny.*

But she didn't say that out loud.

Thunder Sonia was like this with everyone.

She would appear out of nowhere when young elves ran away from home, take them out to have fun, and treat them to meals. She'd then gently admonish the person who'd caused the young elf to run away from home in the first place. Bougainvillea hadn't had that kind of experience herself, but someone in her unit said it happened to him when he was young. Or wait, was he the one who got scolded?

"Don't talk like that. You make it sound like I'm some sort of criminal."

"Well, what is it? If it's something difficult to admit, I won't pry..."

"The other day, I heard about the state of affairs in the succubus country from Lady Carrot. They've been treated poorly by everyone, and their young are starving... I've done some digging these past few days, and it appears she was telling the truth..."

"...Hey, are you planning on going to the country of the succubi?"

"Yes. If I make use of the prestige the name Nazar carries, there ought to be something I can do to help."

"Are you serious? A man walking willy-nilly into succubus country? That's like a mouse strolling into a lion's den! Don't you think you might be underestimating the succubi just a little? You're still young, so you probably don't know much, but succubi... To them, men are just food. You might think you can reason with them, but when they're really hungry and a piece of meat appears, you'll see that they won't be too interested in talking. They're just gonna dig right in..."

"...Oh, I see."

Nazar sighed heavily.

"Does this mean you're part of the problem, Thunder Sonia? Are you just another person who disrespects Lady Carrot and the plight of her people, choosing instead to lean on stereotypes?"

"...Huh?"

Thunder Sonia flinched at the disappointment in Nazar's voice. Damn it, he was handsome, and she definitely had her eye on him as well.

"She was trying to reach a compromise, as a succubus. But you would paint her with the same brush as all the others, never once hearing her concerns?"

"Well... I mean..."

"You must have realized from meeting Lord Bash. Even among the orcs, who only see women as breeding stock, there are still certain individuals capable of respect."

"No, I'm not trying to look down on the succubi. I'm just worried about you..."

But faced with his scolding, Thunder Sonia had no choice but to ultimately fall silent.

Thunder Sonia certainly held a prejudice against the orcs.

Only, meeting Bash had softened that prejudice.

Most orcs may not be so virtuous, but they were still capable of being sensitive and respectful.

If all orcs were like that, she wouldn't mind having one as her husband.

She'd prefer Bash, of course, but she'd already blown it with him by rejecting his proposal. Of course, if he came back for another chance, she'd give it to him.

But Thunder Sonia shook her head. There was no point dwelling on that now.

"Speaking bluntly, where's the proof that Carrot was telling the truth? She may be telling a sob story while secretly kidnapping men behind the scenes."

"Even you don't believe that."

"...Mm, I guess."

The Alliance of Four was famously wary of succubi and demons.

If the succubi were kidnapping men and hatching a nefarious scheme, the Alliance of Four would have long since caught wind of it.

And then they would use that evidence to place sanctions against them. Succubi had to be dealt with firmly after all.

"Ugh..."

Thunder Sonia groaned in frustration.

"Are you done talking? Then I'm leaving."

Nazar began walking away as Thunder Sonia glared at him.

Thunder Sonia frowned, watching him go... But then her expression cooled, and she clapped her hands.

"All right, if that's the case, I'm coming with you!"

Nazar looked back in panic.

"Huh? But you—"

"If I'm there to guard you, no succubus will have the chance to suck out your soul! They may not like it, but this is the best way. Yeah! No need to worry! I, the Great Mage Thunder Sonia, will not let an old war buddy walk into certain death!"

"But, Thunder Sonia..."

"If there's a chance Geddigs will be resurrected, then someone has to go, even if it means investigating the succubi."

Thunder Sonia paused for breath, realizing that Nazar was staring at her.

Then he touched the brim of his hat rakishly.

"Well, this is a surprise. Just don't go catching feelings, though."

Catching feelings? For him?

Thunder Sonia had heard that some women tried to engineer a situation to get a man interested in her. Tactics might include befriending a friend of Nazar's and then seeing if they might introduce her to him. That sort of thing. It was a pretty lame strategy, to be perfectly honest. Her way was better.

"Heh, not a chance."

Of course, there was no way he would see through her playful dismissal. Nazar smiled faintly.

Thunder Sonia took it as encouragement and was just about to continue flirting, when suddenly she became aware of the frowning woman beside her.

"What a face, Bougainvillea. You're coming, too, of course."

"...I am?"

"After that naughty thing you did... You'll be severely punished if you go back to the home country, right? Stay with me until things die down. By the time this trip is over, your period of disgrace should be over and done with."

"Don't need to tell me twice! I'm in!"

"Great! Just the gal I'd like to have in my corner! I'll be counting on you!"

Bougainvillea rubbed her chin thoughtfully.

She really does try to help everyone, not just the elves...

And so Thunder Sonia was on the road again...

...with a man who would never be interested in her, heading to a man-free country populated by creatures who held a strong grudge against her.

Thunder Sonia's path to marriage would continue to be long and fraught with peril.

AFTERWORD

Long time no chat, everyone. Rifujin na Magonote here.

First of all, I would like to take this opportunity to express my gratitude to everyone who picked up the fourth volume of *Orc Eroica*.

Thank you so much, everyone.

Since this is an afterword, I thought I'd write about the various things I struggled with in writing Volume 4, but since I only have a page or two, I'll just talk about my current situation instead.

First of all, I was recently infected with a virus and turned into a zombie!

Zombies are an object of fear. I didn't want to be a zombie and vowed that I would escape this fate. However, I realized being a zombie isn't actually all that bad.

Their bodies are stiff, but they don't have to suffer stiff shoulders. Their brains are simple, which means no stress.

The unbearable appetite is a drawback, of course, but when you think about it, even a human will die if they don't eat, so it's not a big enough issue to waste time worrying about.

So then, here I am, currently wandering around in search of food, using my new simple brain to write novels.

My brain is sluggish, so it takes days to write a single line, but that doesn't matter much because I have an infinite life span. It's kinda like being old forever.

By the way, I'm at a campsite because I know people tend to gather in places like this.

Even though the campsite is far from human settlements, there are supplies and buildings, so it's possible to survive out here. It's the perfect place for a few humans to live in hiding.

I'm fundamentally an indoor person, so I gave up on looking for food by relying on my sense of smell and nonexistent wilderness survival instincts. Instead, I'm just waiting around for someone to show up. I kill time by lighting fires, gazing at the starry sky, and writing novels.

To use some terminology from my human days, it's sort of like a hybrid method of hunting, utilizing camouflage in tandem with an ant lion pit.

Humans are surprisingly easy to trap this way. The campsite shows signs of human activity, not zombie activity. Therefore, there are no zombies here.

It's ironic that someone like me, an indoor person, would have ended up going camping. The tactics I'm using are a little bit underhanded as well, but whatever...

Even so, ahhh, the crackling bonfire, the mountains at night, the blissful silence, the clear air, it all seems to cleanse my body and mind. It makes me wonder why I never tried camping before becoming a zombie.

As I write this, it seems that humans have finally arrived.

Welp, it's dinner time. Let's do this.

Sorry, I got off track... To Asanagi, who drew such wonderful illustrations for this volume. To K, the editor in charge (I'm sorry I caused you so much inconvenience, what with me being so distracted by my work on *Jobless Reincarnation*) and to all the other people who were involved in this book... Not to mention, to all the readers who are always waiting for the next volume...

Thank you very much for everything this time around as well. See you again in Volume 5.

Rifujin na Magonote